Vanessa Alexander lives in Essex with her family. She is a keen historian and full-time writer.

THE LOVE KNOT

Spring, 1297. Edward I's fury is unbounded when he discovers proof of the clandestine affair of his daughter, Joanna of Acre, with penniless commoner Ralph Monthermer. He immures Joanna in a nunnery, and only the intervention of Henry Trokelowc, Edward's clerk, prevents him from killing Ralph, who is imprisoned in Bristol Castle while Henry investigates. To the lovers, the only proof of the other's continued existence is a series of intense, coded letters. Their only chance of survival lies in Henry Trokelowe's hands. But how can a confirmed bachelor even begin to understand their all-consuming passion?

VANESSA

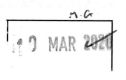
THE LOVE KNOT

Complete and Unabridged

ULVERSCROFT

First published in Great Britain in 1999 by
Headline Book Publishing
London

First Large Print Edition
published 2000
by arrangement with
Headline Book Publishing
a division of
Hodder Headline Plc
London

British Library CIP Data

Alexander, Vanessa
    The love knot.—Large print ed.—
    Ulverscroft large print series: romance
    1. Great Britain—History—Edward I, *1272 –
    1307* —Fiction 2. Historical fiction
    3. Large type books
    I. Title
    823.9'14 [F]

    ISBN 0–7089–4314–4

Published by
F. A. Thorpe (Publishing)
Anstey, Leicestershire
Set by Words & Graphics Ltd.
Anstey, Leicestershire
Printed and bound in Great Britain by
T. J. International Ltd., Padstow, Cornwall

This book is printed on acid-free paper

To CLC
With TLC

Introduction

This novel is set in 1297 when the widowed Edward I, King of England, was trying to establish his rule over Wales and Scotland. Edward used his children as pawns on the diplomatic marriage chessboard; he expected duty rather than love to be the first consideration of his offspring. In 1297 the King faced a fierce conflict of wills with his impetuous daughter Joanna, the widowed Countess of Gloucester, who fell deeply in love with a humble knight, Sir Ralph Monthermer.

Letter 1

To Ralph Monthermer, prisoner, but captor of my heart, Joanna of England sends her deepest love.

I have written my first line yet now I want to stop. I will surely die if I do not see your face again. I did not know my eyes could cry so many tears or my heart feel so cold without you. I think only of you, I dream only of you, I desire only you. I gave my life to you as soon as I saw you. I was born to be yours. I have spoken my passion to you. My eyes arc witness to it. My heart sings of it. My soul treasures it. Now my hand writes it, yet poorly so, for true love and deep passion have no words. I am lost in the valley of the restless mind. My life is clouded by your absence. Oh, I miss you! Only the fierceness of your passion, the sweet kiss of your lips can release me. I would give up everything I am, everything I was, everything I shall be, for just one more day with you.

I am Joanna, Princess of England, daughter of the great Edward, Countess of Gloucester, a seigneur in my own right, but I would surrender it all to be with you. I have taken your love. I have it within me. Your life is now mine. My soul follows yours. Our lives are entangled, never to be separated. Your very shadow is more pleasing to me than the fullness of the air. I wake with you. I live with you. I dream with you. I am no longer myself but a new creation. I am not what I was but what you have made me. To be parted from you, to be kept prisoner from your presence, dulls the most fiery preacher's description of Hell.

Yesterday, just before midnight, I woke from a sweat-soaked sleep. My heart knew new terrors. Were you alive? Were you suffering? Were you thinking of me or lost in your own dreams? I floundered upon my bed, casting about for you, but there was nothing, only the creak of ancient wood, the distant sounds of the convent, the scurry of mice and the faint call of some night bird echoing from the great oaks which ring the convent. I never dreamt this silent, hallowed place could hold such terror. To be alone is to be dead! To be separated from my beloved is to be in Hell. I could not sleep. I opened the shutters and looked out on the same sky you must stare up at. The moon was full. Below me lay the cloister garth, its grass drenched in a silver light.

I pretended you were there, waiting for me

as you have often waited for me. I could bear it no longer. I left my chamber and slipped down the stairs. Old Mother Beatrice, the porter, snored in her wine-sodden sleep. The door to the gardens was unlocked. The air was cold but I was warm, pretending you were with me. I walked across the grass. All around me danced the shadows of the cloisters. I ignored them. In the centre of the garth grows a rose bush, its tangled greenness protected by spikes. At the top bloomed one red rose, its petals open to the full moon. I touched it gently and remembered the rose you dropped in my lap in the love-knot garden at Westminster. One simple touch and I was back there. My mind was filled with colour. The sun's warmth thawed the chill in my heart and I was looking up into your smiling eyes. Around us the court swirled like a coloured river. On that day I felt a ripple of flame course through my soul, which rages more fiercely every day.

I sat by my rose and cried again. I clawed at the earth for what I once had and what I now miss. I prayed, then I laughed because, from the convent stables, a horse whinnied — an eerie sound on the cold night air. I opened my eyes and, believe me, all had changed. Before me stretched the tournament ground at Wallingford with its coloured barrier of taffeta and gorgeous cloths and the silken pavilions of my father and his barons. Pennants and banners, scarlet and gold, kissed the breeze and fluttered bravely. The final joust was about to begin. Father held my hand. I dared not look at you lest my eyes played the Judas to my heart. Oh, I felt your eyes on me. Even from where I sat I could sense you and touch, yet again, the token of love I had secretly given you.

On that day of all days, I kept my eyes down, my lips closed. The trumpets sounded, the heralds shouted and threw their staffs into the air.

'Joanna!' my father exclaimed. 'Look now, Monthermer is ready!'

I glanced the other way, at your opponent Humphrey de Bohun, waiting at the far end of the lists, gorgeous in his armour and brilliant display of banners. A squire was offering him his tilting helm, on its top the carving of a boar's head. Its tusks gleamed cruelly in the sunlight and I became afraid. You were waiting at the other end, the champion of my heart, preparing for the final run. A trumpet brayed, or was it more? I cannot remember. I closed my eyes. I could hear the drumming hooves as you and de Bohun closed. The beat of hooves grew so loud I wondered if it was my heart.

My father exclaimed and shook my hand. I still held his and my nails were digging deep into his calloused skin.

'Joanna,' he whispered. 'What is the matter?'

I opened my eyes and held his gaze even at the clash of arms and the shrill neigh of the horses. My eyes betrayed me. My father knew. Yet at the time he did not look angry but sad; his light-blue eyes filled with tears. Gently he freed my hand.

'He has won,' he said. 'Your Ralph has won.'

I looked up. You were before me, seated on your horse. Your battered shield hung from the saddle horn, the visor of your helmet was up. The victor, the King's own champion! I knew what was coming. My eyes begged you to be careful but how could you know? The victor's crown, the laurel wreath, was on the tip of your lance. I prayed to all the saints I knew and even those I did not. But what can stop love except love itself? The lance came down towards me, the chaplet of flowers on its tip. You wished to crown me queen of the tournament.

I could not move. It is not that I lack courage or the passion to love. I just found myself trapped, my arms turned to stone, my fingers heavy as lead. Father moved.

He plucked the chaplet from your lance and placed it on my head. Oh, everyone cheered but I saw Father's eyes and I blushed. I, Joanna, Princess of England, Countess of Gloucester, blushed like a novice nun. My cheeks burned. My heart throbbed.

God knows, that day you captured it completely. I have never told you this before because you may have mistaken me. It was not fear of the King or what he might do. No, from that moment I knew that my love was the only thing that mattered. And so the die was cast.

Last night the cold breeze eventually dispelled my vision. All that was left was a lonely moon-washed cloister and a red rose stretching up to the sky, like I reach out to you. I moved closer to my rose. I ignored the thorns and kissed its soft, sweet petals. I whispered to it, as I would whisper into the ear of your heart, how much I loved you. I kissed that rose and prayed the breeze would carry my message to you.

I have not been able to write before. Let me tell you about my prison. The convent of St Mary at Malmesbury rests among quiet woods and serene fields. It is not really a prison, more a place of refuge; the real pain is being separated from you and deep fears for the future. The convent's Abbess, the Lady

Emma, has eyes of ice and is as formidable as any bishop. She treats me with cold courtesy. She grudgingly acknowledges my status but leaves me in no doubt of my present position. I am in her charge, subject to her rules and discipline. She smiles with her lips but her eyes remain constant in their frostiness. We share wine, nibble on marchpane, discuss the doings of the convent or the gossip from the court, little else. I do not blame her. She is under strict orders from the King. I have decided to play the part and hide my passion. I give her no cause for concern. She does not hear the terrible roaring in my heart. She knows nothing of those dark days after I was plucked from your life by soldiers in armour: the rasp of steel; the glowing pitch torches in shadowy stairwells; the whispered commands and the harsh orders. The chill night air froze my skin as I was bundled onto a horse and hurried along midnight roads. So, I am modest and moderate here. A woman coming to her senses, rather than one who has lost all reason and finds life robbed of meaning. The Lady Abbess patronises me and doles out news like she would bread to the poor. I have learnt how you, too, were taken and brought to Bristol Castle. I pray God my father treats you gently.

I am sorry if you think I betrayed you. I

did not. I write to tell you of my love but also to confirm that our great secret is safe. It is locked fast in my heart. No lawyer, clerk, priest or knight will ever prise it loose. So, I beg you, whatever happens, sharpen your wits. Do not tell anyone what we both treasure. Do not betray me or my father's rage will know no bounds. It will mean exile, even death for you, and if you die, I will live no longer. I write now urgently, my quill skims across the parchment. I use the cipher known only to us, the secret way I taught you, not only to send my love but to warn and advise you what has happened.

Since my arrival at Malmesbury I have reflected on how it all began. Spring is now well gone but it was winter, the snow was falling, when my father, the King, arrived at Tonbridge. He arrived unexpectedly, the way he always does, banners flying, horsemen around him. The great Edward of England sitting high in the saddle, staring down at me as he used to when I was a child and Mother told me to offer him the posset cup before a day's hunting. His murrey tunic was coated with mud and the trackway dirt caked his boots and clogged his spurs. I met him in the castle bailey. Oh, thanks be to God, you were not there! Father came just before dawn, his heralds thundering across the drawbridge, shouting, 'The King, make way for the King!' I was in my chamber, Alicia behind me dressing my hair. I grabbed a fur and wrapped it about my shoulders. Alicia looked terrified, face pale, eyes dark and round. I pressed my finger against her lips.

'Hush!' I said. 'The only traitor here is fear.'

Poor Alicia! God knows what has happened to her. When they took me I screamed her name. I have written to my father to punish me, if he thinks fit, but not my servants. On that mist-filled morning Alicia thought the same as I, that the King had come to trap me, but Father is not like that. He would not tiptoe up the stairs and stand like a pimp outside my chamber door. By the time I reached the bailey I felt guilty at such a thought. Edward of England stared down at me, and my guilt only deepened. He looked older, his face more lined and marked. The golden moustache and beard which, when I was a child, he used to brush against my face to make me squeal, were faded and streaked with silver. His great hand came down and cupped my chin.

'Joanna,' he smiled. 'I am here and I am freezing in the saddle.'

I remembered myself. I knelt and kissed his hand. He urged me up and then dismounted, quick and agile as any young squire.

Does he know? I wondered. Had his spies been busy? Since Wallingford he had never looked askance at me but, at that moment, my heart skipped a beat, my belly quivered. I froze from a frost which came from within rather than the cutting dawn breeze. Does he suspect? His eyes held mine then drifted away. I glanced around. My dead husband's two black crows, Tibault the seneschal and Ricaud the priest, were standing like harbingers of doom on the steps of the keep.

'Father, you are most welcome,' I said and kissed him on the cheek.

The King changed in the twinkling of an eye. He gathered me up in a gust of sweat, perfume and leather.

'In widow's weeds,' he whispered. 'The Lord be my witness, Joanna, you remind me of Eleanor.'

'You still grieve, Father?'

'Not a second passes,' he murmured before releasing me, 'not a beat of the heart but I remember her.' He stood back and looked at me from head to toe. Then he clapped his hands. 'But we are here among the living,' he roared, grinning at his retinue. 'I have come to enjoy myself with my daughter.'

And so he did, as of old — except these

days he cares little about his appearance. He rarely changed his clothes and never washed but rose before dawn in whatever he was dressed in, and went down to the castle chapel where Ricaud said the Mass as usual. Father would click his tongue if the priest preached too long, or even dictated letters and memoranda for the Chancery in London in a loud whisper to the clerk sitting next to him. He would take Christ's body and drink his blood, then clap his hands and hasten down the courtyard to where the hunt was waiting. Dogs yapped, horses neighed, their breath rising like clouds of incense to the sky. Falconers talked softly to their hooded birds. Scullions from the kitchen served slabs of roasted meat from a platter and cups of claret heated with a red-hot poker. Father would eat as if he'd fasted for days and then he'd saddle up. Even then he would be doing three things at once, checking the falcons were fine and the huntsmen had their instructions, while hurriedly dictating some letter to a red-nosed clerk. One morning he caught my eye.

'The Scots are in rebellion!' he roared. 'Wallace is burning my towns! I need good men on the northern march, like young Ralph, eh?'

I stared coolly back. Father turned away

and, with the hunt galloping behind him, charged across the drawbridge, down to the mist-shrouded marshes to fly his falcons against the heron and stork. Late in the afternoon he would return: another Mass, more business then boisterous feasting and drinking. I watched him, all bluster and false gaiety.

The royal baggage train arrived three days after him; with it came a gaggle of young choristers whom he was training to sing the divine chant and the psalter. Earls and barons also came to discuss the war in Scotland. They spent noisy, raucous afternoons in the solar poring over maps, drinking wine, shouting and roaring at each other. The clerks set up a chancery office high in the keep and the castle reeked with the smell of incense, burning wax, ink and the dust from scrubbed parchments.

I am so glad you were not there. Oh, I missed you! Every soul has its hymn and you are mine but I sensed danger. Edward my father may be King but he is also an actor without equal. He wandered the castle like a child at Yuletide looking for presents hidden away. He talked to this person and that, especially to those two sharp-eyed crows Tibault and Ricaud, but never to Alicia. I was fooled, like I always am. I love my father and the longer he stayed, the more his charm lulled me. We feasted and made merry every evening. My father himself went down to the kitchens, lecturing the cooks on damson quinces and almond omelettes, how to roll meat and berries in pastries, the best way to prepare fruit fritters or lace pears with carob cream. One night he pushed the cooks aside and cooked salmon in white wine sauce and poached calves with mustard slices for me and his guests. His jesters and tumblers entertained us. Tom the fool and Mathilda Make-Merry cavorted and danced for us in the great hall. The wine flowed and Father would grow nostalgic. At the end of the meal he would sit back in his chair and take my hand, like he did at the tournament at Wallingford. 'Joanna of Acre,' he declared one evening. 'That's what we called you. Look at you with your brown eyes and your blonde hair. Who'd think you were born Outre-Mer?' He slurped his wine. I knew what was coming.

'I nearly died there, little one. If I have told you the story before, I apologise. Your mother and I were on crusade. Eleanor was the fairest woman the Holy Land had seen, apart from God's own Mother, and I was her warrior prince. The Old Man of the Mountains sent an assassin after me; he got through my guards and stabbed me deep with a poisoned knife. You were a child wrapped in swaddling. Your mother, Joanna, picked up a dagger, cut the wound and sucked the poison from me.' He would drum his fingers on the table. 'And look at you now, Joanna. The widow of a great earl.' He squeezed my hand. 'You had a happy life, did you not, with Gilbert the Red Earl? A good man, a stern warrior.'

Father had never loved my former husband in life so why in death? I wondered. Down memory lane he led me, and round and round like a dancer in the garden he spun me, sometimes mourning the death of young Alfonso his eldest son, sometimes reliving joyful moments with his Queen, my mother.

One night we left the hall and went up to the Chamber of Shadows in the east tower. I had never been there since that freezing December night when my late husband's corpse was found, blue-faced and staring-eyed, at the bottom of the steps: Father talked about his death. What was Earl Gilbert doing? How was his mood? Did he slip? Who found the body? That was the only time I mentioned your name and, when I did, my father turned away, his right eyelid drooping. I should have heeded the signs but a daughter's love for her father is apt to blind her. He was Edward of England, tall and muscular, jouster extraordinaire, horseman without rival, warrior and crusader. The premier knight who used to gather me up in his arms when I was a child and dance with me before all his court.

He'd often walk with me, late in the evening, along the castle walls. We'd stand and watch the mist creep in. All the time he talked like a priest at confession. In reality he was what he is, a warrior laying siege, taking a castle by stealth rather than by storm. He discussed my life as the Red Earl's wife. Sometimes my tongue itched to tell him all. Then he'd sense my melancholy and grasp my hand.

'Let me tell you about Tom the Fool,' he smiled. 'Do you remember when Cardinal Peter the Spaniard came to court? I wined and dined him. I talked and cooed to sweeten both him and his master in Rome. Anyway,' my father turned, elbow resting against the wall, 'I sent the good cardinal back to Dover with the Earl of Lincoln and told Tom to accompany them. A day later a messenger, one of Tom's friends, arrived. He announced that Tom had died.'

'Died?' I queried. 'He's alive and well!'

'No, no, listen!' My father held back his laughter. 'The messenger brought strict instructions for Tom's mistress. It was Tom's final wish that she should immediately move in with the messenger who brought the news of his death. And so she did. Three weeks later Tom returned, alive and well, to find his friend had taken full joy of his mistress.' My father clapped his hands. 'Tom had his revenge. He discovered that the source of the joke was the Earl of Lincoln. As you know, Tom is skilled in languages. Anyway, a Spanish abbess visited the court, a kinswoman of your mother's. The Earl of Lincoln didn't know Spanish so Tom wrote him a speech.' My father laughed. 'The abbess fainted when she heard it. Tom's speech for the Earl was one of the filthiest stories anyone had ever heard.'

He laughed again and kissed me on the cheek. This was the father I loved, amusing and charming. In reality the net was closing, the trap was being prepared. On the eve of Candlemas he sprung the trap.

The day's feasting was over; we were playing chess when he plucked at my sleeve.

'Come.' He smiled, took me by the hand and led me up to the castle chapel. 'I want to pray for Eleanor,' he said, 'and tell you news.'

He lit the candles and sat on the altar steps, saying that Jesus wouldn't mind if kings treated each other with mutual courtesy. I sat on a stool. My father glanced up . . .

I'll tell you no more, not for the moment.

Night is falling. Darkness laps like water across the grass, stretching out to blind my windows. My love, we must be prudent, coupling the cunning of the serpent with the innocence of the dove.

This letter will be given to Rosstal, a merchant who supplies the convent with certain provisions. The Lady Abbess agreed that I may send it with him and he will bring the letter to you. I do not know why such permission has been given. Is it to trap us? But, if this is the only way to touch your life, how can I refuse? They will undoubtedly break the seal but can they break the cipher? Read it well and, if you can reply, be most prudent. Grieve with me but not for me. If God is love, and love cannot be checked, then all will be well. Like water, love will find its own path or, like sunlight, pierce the smallest crack or crevice.

In a way I am glad I am here; better the chatter of the sisters than the jibes and sneers of court. Each day here has its own measure, a slow rhythm but a rhythm nonetheless. I have had to assume the dress, but not the vows, of the good sisters. On that first dreadful night my

19

father's men cut my hair. 'It is the custom of this convent,' the Lady Abbess declared primly, 'that the hair of those who enter our community is cut by whoever brings them to this house. You are no different.' I wear a wimple white as snow and the blue veil and gown of a nun but, God knows, I am yours. My vows are to you. The Abbess has given me a book of hours. The prayers are dead words, except for one phrase from the Psalms. I murmur it as I fall asleep: 'I desire thee like a deer seeks water in a parched land.'

The Lady Abbess has also sent me a book, *The Four Seasons of Man*, in which a preacher claims that women should not learn to write! A woman should, he claims, be schooled to be as dull as mud and bereft of all learning so that she is unable to write love letters. When I read it I laughed for the first time since I was taken. I wished I could share it with you, as we did all our secrets, in my chamber, when the fire burnt merrily, the logs cracked and the spiced posset cup warmed our hearts. Oh, such times! I thought my heart would shatter at the happiness which ravished it. Such thoughts comfort me now.

I join the sisters in their devotions: matins, lauds and prime. In my arrogance I dismissed them as gutted candles with shrivelled breasts and dry, cracked wombs but, as I shall tell you, they are kind and merry. Old women in the main, their husbands long dead, they now spend their widowhood with each other and God, though fashion dies hard. They wear coral brooches and silver clasps and nurse their lap dogs which they feed with manchet bread soaked in milk and honey. Few visit them, their families put them here then forget them. They are too proud to show their pain and conceal their loneliness in endless chatter. They look for humour in all things. They know about me but keep their peace, though they pluck at my sleeve and smile sadly. Like them, I seek to be merry, to be a true soldier and hide my pain. The Lady Abbess makes us eat in silence while one of the good sisters reads from the lectern. Two nights ago a story was recited, a pious warning to widows about the wiles of men. Afterwards, at recreation, the old sisters clustered about me, fearful that the reading was directed at me.

'Do not worry,' clucked Sister Agnes. Her vein-streaked hand stroked my cheek. 'What does the Lady Abbess really know about the wiles of men?'

'And what do you?' broke in Sister

Veronica, an old, wizened crone who loudly proclaims she has had six husbands and keeps their embalmed, shrivelled hearts in caskets in her room.

'I know enough,' Sister Agnes replied. 'I have been married four times. My second husband was a physician.'

'And?' the good sisters chorused, sensing a story.

Sister Agnes's head came forward like a little sparrow's. 'He couldn't make love,' she whispered, 'unless it was raining outside.'

'What did you do?' the chorus asked.

'I asked a friend to climb on the roof every night and pour water down the window.'

'And?' Sister Veronica demanded.

'The poor man died of exhaustion.'

The good sisters shrieked with laughter. Their humour is powerful medicine.

Oh, heart of my heart, I miss you. Sometimes I look up, out of my window, and see you, the hawk of my heart swooping towards me. You have grasped my soul and hold my life in your tender grip. I will go wherever you take me. I will not write any more, not for a while, not till I know that this letter has reached you. Keep our secret, be brave and resolute! Remember this: three things are constant — the greenness of the earth, the rising of the sun and my love for you.

Written at Malmesbury, the feast of St Catherine, April 1297.

Letter 2

Henry Trokelowe, senior clerk in the Royal Chapel, sends his Grace, Edward the King, health and blessings.

Your Grace, I am flattered you have entrusted this delicate task to me. I am, as Your Grace knows, your most faithful servant. At our meeting in the Chamber of the Green Cloth, Westminster, you praised the commentary I had written on Constantine the African's treatise on lovesickness from his great work *The Viaticum*. This was, I confess, no more than a folly of my more callow days in the Halls of Oxford. In truth, I am untutored in matters of love. At thirty-seven years of age I am still a bachelor. I have not loved and lost a woman's heart so I cannot truly understand the pain, or the joy, of the troubadours' songs. Some would say I am as cold as a cod in ice. My skill, such as it is, lies in logic, and logic and love are incompatible. Love knows no reason, cannot be measured, weighed or analysed. Love causes chaos. Logic, however, imposes order, and in this present business logic will root out the facts, proclaim the truth, and see justice done.

Your Grace's daughter is infatuated with a commoner, Ralph Monthermer. You likened her infatuation to a Gordian knot which should be cut out with the slash of a sword. I advised against this. The Lady Joanna is your daughter and, may I say, Your Grace, a reflection of your own temperament and humour. She is self-willed, strong-headed and resolute; once her mind is fixed on a matter, her will cannot be brooked. She is twenty-five years of age, no milksop maid mewling under the moon but the widow of Sir Gilbert de Clare, well described as the Red Earl, a man of steel and fiery temperament.

Undoubtedly she loves Ralph Monthermer, three years her junior, a commoner but, according to report, a keen swordsman and a brave warrior. Love is a paradox, or so I am led to believe; it often hurts and the more it does, the greater love grows until one cannot distinguish what is more important, the love or the hurt it causes. I mention this, Your Grace, not to preach but to urge caution in this matter, to unpick this love knot carefully.

Lord Gilbert died on the 7th of December 1295 some sixteen months ago. Common gossip has it that your daughter and her squire, whom you knighted at her request, were chamber friends before Earl Gilbert died. Of course, as Your Grace knows, friendship does not mean adultery nor does it prove murder. Earl Gilbert allegedly died from a fall down the stairs outside the 'Chamber of Shadows' at Tonbridge Castle. Was he pushed? Did our two lovers conspire secretly to bring about his death and hasten his journey into eternity? This is the question you wish answered. I shall interrogate, both the Lady Joanna and Sir Ralph, but in a subtle way. I would strongly advise against rough handling; the grip of the pincers, the heat of the branding iron, the pain of the pulley and the rack might break their bodies but it will not touch their souls, and it is from their souls that the truth will come.

We must watch and wait. I am, as Your Grace knows, a keen fisherman. I have no greater joy in life than to take my small boat from King's Steps at Westminster and go downriver with rod and line to sit and fish near a reedy bank, where the fish are plentiful and fat. All clerks should do some fishing. To wait and watch, to exercise great patience, sharpens the wit. In this matter we must, as the Latin puts it, *festina lente* — hasten slowly. Let the gossips wag their tongues. Let the world think what it wishes. In trying to control slander we might as well strive to catch moonbeams in a jar.

Yesterday morning, after I attended Mass in the church of St Mary-le-Bow, I finished my prayers, lit a candle before the Virgin and left. I knew a group of powerful aldermen had espied me there. They were clustered further down Cheapside but their leader, Sir Peter Philpott, came scurrying up the steps.

'Good morrow, Sir Peter,' I said. 'I trust you are well?'

'And you, Master Henry,' he replied. 'You are fresh from Westminster?'

'I am from Westminster,' I responded, 'but whether I am fresh or not is a matter for my barber.'

He laughed, hiding yellow teeth behind dirty fingers. 'We have heard rumours, Master Henry, about the Lady Joanna, the King's daughter.' He drew closer, his face all concern. 'She is taken, and so is her lover, Sir Ralph Monthermer. They say the King's anger knows no bounds.'

'Why, Sir Peter,' I replied, 'if I knew the King's mind, then I would be King. That would be treason and you would be a party to it!'

He scurried away.

So, Your Grace, the news is out but let it run its course. I'll hook the truth and bring it to you fresh.

After meeting Sir Peter I broke my fast in a cookshop and, within the hour, I joined my escort and took the Pilgrim's Way into Kent. I thought it best to visit Tonbridge, to cast about and stir the dirty pool to see what manner of things came floating to the top. The castle itself was quiet. Its Constable, Matthew Hinkley, met me, hands all aflutter, like a chicken visited by the fox. Our horses were stabled and he gave me a chamber in the gatehouse.

'Leave me be,' I told him when we dined in the great hall that evening. 'Let me move quietly around and capture the substance.'

He didn't understand. 'What do you mean, sir?' he murmured. 'Capture the substance?'

'Why, Master Matthew,' I replied, 'the business of Lady Joanna and Sir Ralph.'

Immediately I knew which side of the line he would stand.

'The Lady Joanna is a gracious lady.' He drew himself up, fingering the buttons on his jerkin.

Aye, I thought, you would think that. You are a simple soul. A lady's smile and a silver coin would make you look the other way.

'Was there anything scandalous in their relationship?'

'If there was,' he said stiffly, 'I did not know of it.'

And if you did, you wouldn't tell, I thought.

'I know nothing,' he protested. He pushed his stool away and got to his feet. 'I have duties to attend to.' He walked towards the door.

'Master Matthew!' I called out.

He turned.

'I carry the King's warrant and do the King's will in this matter. In future, only leave when I tell you I have finished with you!'

He slammed the door behind him. Ah well, I thought, there goes an enemy. He will tell the rest to be on their guard but that is what I intended. His warnings would bring the divisions within the castle to light. Those who support the Lady Joanna would keep their lips closed while those with something to say would scurry forward all the faster. I had already met the seneschal, Tibault, and the castle chaplain, Ricaud, and regarded them as two ripe plums, ready to drop into my hands.

I left the hall and ordered a servant to take me to the Lady Joanna's chamber. The door was locked but Hinkley was fetched and at my command broke the seals and let me in. He tried to follow. I gave like for like and slammed the door in his face.

I mention these petty details, Your Grace, because he and others of his choir will no doubt be singing a hymn of complaint which will reach you at Westminster.

In accordance with your instructions, the chamber had not been touched. I crouched for a while before the fire grate. Here, as you told me, on the night she was taken, Lady Joanna burnt some papers. Nothing remains but feathery, blackened ash, cold and crumbling to the touch. I opened the shutters and looked around. Darkness was falling. I struck a tinder and lit some candles. The chests and coffers contained linen cloths, dresses, collars and bracelets — nothing untoward. I would recommend, however, that the precious jewels be taken to Your Grace's treasure house in Westminster.

The scent of herbs was strong in the clothing, as might be expected since Lady Joanna would not have worn any of them for some time, being in widow's weeds since her husband's death. The four-poster bed had a golden tester over it and a coverlet decorated with fleur-de-lys and the leopards of England. I pulled this back. As I did so, I noticed a stain on the left side and took the coverlet over to the window. I am not sure but I think it was blood. Some attempt had been made to wash it out but this had failed — as Martha my laundry woman could have told whoever made the attempt. 'All stains can come out,' she says, 'except blood. It's as if God wishes it to stay as a witness to this or to that.' Strange how one collects wisdom, is it not?

I ran my hands beneath the bolster. I found a rosary, plain and simple with a silver cross, and also a dagger with a razor edge and a pin-like tip. Its handle was carved with rings for the fingers. I understand why the Lady Joanna would sleep with a rosary to hand, but a dagger? I picked it up and held it in my hands. It was more like a bodkin than a knife.

It is the small things which betray, the little items overlooked. I sat in the window seat; its cushion is thick and quilted. I put the dagger down and it slid down the side of the cushion, so I moved the cushion to retrieve the knife, and noticed herbs there, dried and crackling. You told me the Lady Joanna was skilled in herb craft and loved her garden. At first I thought the herbs had been sprinkled to sweeten the air. I, too, have some knowledge of herbs. I gathered some up between my fingers and smelt horehound, fennel, comfrey. I went to the smaller window, a mere arrow slit, and removed its shutter. More herbs were sprinkled in the lintel, and I found the same on either side of the door. I wondered why the Lady Joanna would sprinkle herbs near every opening to her chamber. Do not the wise women recommend such herbs to keep the ghosts of the dead at bay?

A small crucifix was nailed to the wall above the door, and pushed behind it was a piece of the palm which is blessed and distributed on Palm Sunday. What, I asked myself, was the Lady Joanna fearful of? The ghost of her dead husband? I heard noises in the gallery outside so I bolted the door, took off my cloak and belt and conducted a more thorough search.

The Lady Joanna was arrested at night by your guards. She had little time to hide anything; her attempts to do so would have been clumsy and hurried. I cleaned out the grate and discovered nothing, but in a corner of the inglenook I found a silver ring which I enclose with this letter. It is simple enough. However, if Your Grace examines it closely, you will find engraved on the inner rim the letters 'R.M.' and 'J. of G.' — Ralph Monthermer and Joanna of Gloucester. Did Your Grace ever notice this on the Lady Joanna's hand? I suspect she was wearing it on the night she was taken. She must have plucked it from her finger and cast it away.

I searched on. Among her clothing I found a dry garland of flowers wrapped in cloth of silk to preserve it. The flowers were not truly faded so the wreath must have been fashioned within the last twelvemonth. Why should a widow, grieving for her husband, wear, and carefully preserve, a chaplet of flowers? I also uncovered a lady's glove fashioned out of calfskin and studded with jewels on the back. The other, I understand, was found concealed in Monthermer's jerkin when he was taken by your guards. I must go through the castle accounts and discover when those gloves were purchased so as to establish when your daughter could have given the other of the pair to Sir Ralph as a token. Your Grace, I am uneasy. I sift through the possessions of a princess of England. In the darkened chamber, with the night falling, I began to wonder what had really happened on the night Earl Gilbert died. I must ask myself a number of questions.

First, is the love between the Lady Joanna and Sir Ralph innocent? Did it begin before Lord Gilbert's death as one of those chivalrous accords between a lady and one of her husband's knights so adored by the troubadours and minstrels? Or did the Lady Joanna and Sir Ralph play the two-backed beast together — if Your Grace will pardon the expression? If their love was adulterous, was it also malicious and murderous in intent?

True, I am an expert on Constantine the African's treatise on lovesickness. I know there is more to 'amour' than tavern songs or courtly romances. The poets talk of love's castle being bombarded by roses, of bodies and souls being linked by fair glances. But love is also a madness and, like a madcap, requires a dark house and a whip for correction. Out of love can spin hate, and the deeper the love, the greater the malice it can engender. Did not Lucifer, when he fell from the star-shot heavens, transmute, in his own diabolical way, his love of God into hatred of all things divine?

I sat on a small stool within the doorway of that chamber. I watched the pale light shafting through the window and wondered if the love between Lady Joanna and her knight gave birth to a monster called 'Murder'. A poet's fancy, one of your courtiers might say, but I have stood in the battle line, not only with your forces in Wales and Scotland but also in those invisible fights created and nourished by the human heart, and I have looked through the windows of men's souls and glimpsed the dark shadows and phantasms lurking within.

Seated in that chamber I heard footsteps along the gallery outside, followed by a knock on the door which I ignored. I walked across to the window. Why is it that people, and especially lovers, like to stand at a window and stare out? What is it about windows which provokes a spark in the souls of lovers? Do they think that by gazing out, they can somehow reach their beloved? Does it give peace to the mind and allow the soul to travel where it wishes? I felt along the window frame, searching for crevices between the wood and the hard stone. Most were too small for my fingers so I drew my dagger and probed more deeply. First I drew out a fillet which a young lady may use to tie her hair.

What's this? I asked myself. Why would a widow, whose hair hangs long and lovely, need a fillet to keep it in place? And why should the ribbon be hidden away? Next I found a dry and cracked piece of holly entwined with ivy. This was more telling for it symbolises lovers. Was the Lady Joanna the holly and Sir Ralph Monthermer the ivy, winding himself round both her body and her soul? Why hide them away? Not from the eyes of Your Grace's soldiers or clerks surely, but because they were a precious possession, a keepsake of happier times. Lastly I found a scrap of parchment, rolled up tightly. On it was written this poem:

The blood doesn't flow so freely now,
Caked thickly in her veins,
When before, free and liquid it could
    pass
To every part of her body.
She stands by the mirror.
Her face reflects past storms and cares.
She taps the side of her head.
'In here,' she murmurs, 'the demons
    lurk.'
Passions beat about her head,
Vengeance curling like a snake ready to
    strike,
The fires seethe within her.
Past wrongs piled like a heap of filthy
    rubbish
Waiting to be burned.
She hears her child call from the foot
    of the stairs,
A plaintive plea. Her heart bursts with
    anger
But she smiles and pats her head.
Behind her the root of evil,
Her husband wine-merry in the evening,
A Judas without compassion.
No gallows high for him
For the blood-money.

Cast down in the temple of her heart,
The child cries.
She looks again.
Love's dead
Memories sweet?
Nothing new,
Just ice-cold,
Blackened ash.

I have copied it carefully. It is in your
daughter's hand. The parchment is old,
yellowing, dry as a fallen leaf, so it was
written some time ago. Yet the words jump
out at you. They claw at your heart and
catch your breath. I have read and re-read
this poem. If one of Your Grace's clever
sergeants-at-law took this before the King's
Bench, I have no doubt that any judge would
conclude that the Lady Joanna has a case to
answer for the death of her husband. The
poem is filled with desolation. What are
these past wrongs? Why is her husband
described as a Judas without compassion,
worthy of death? And her own relationship
with him is dismissed as ice-cold, blackened
ash. No date is given, no indication of when
it was written. I wonder if the Lady Joanna
composed it before she met Sir Ralph. Was
her heart so empty it could be so easily filled?
Was she so vulnerable that her senses were

ravished by his gentle words, soft touches, deep sighs and longing glances? And yet is she the victim? Or the cause?

When I met Your Grace in your secret chamber at Westminster you intimated that Monthermer might have bewitched your daughter's heart and led her soul astray. Your lawyers would seize on this poem and cry, 'It is all the evidence we need.' But is it? I believe it tells more of your daughter than it does of Monthermer.

I left the chamber and found Constable Hinkley lurking like a ghost in the darkened gallery. He approached, more deferential than the last time we met.

'Master Henry, you are satisfied?'

'Master Matthew,' I retorted, 'my appetite has only been whetted.'

I plucked him by the sleeve and made him sit in the cushioned window seat which overlooks the inner courtyard of the castle. I had placed the items I had found in the Lady Joanna's chamber in a Chancery bag and kept it between my feet. I could see from his eyes, as well as the way his fingers itched, how he wondered what I had discovered.

'Do not vex yourself,' I told him. 'The truth will out eventually. You called the Lady Joanna gracious.'

'Yes I did and so she is.' He smiled but his eyelids blinked.

'Why are you so nervous, Master Matthew?' I asked. 'Regard me as a priest and this as a confessional. Let me hear your thoughts, then I'll shrive you and the King will bless you.' I tapped the purse strung to my belt and the coins clinked like little bells within.

'What is it you want to know?' he stammered.

'The truth.'

'About what?'

'Why, the Lady Joanna and Sir Ralph Monthermer.' I could tell a great fear was on him for the sweat broke out on his brow.'

'Let me help you.' I felt like Lucifer whispering into some poor soul's ear. 'In the autumn of the year twelve hundred and ninety-five, on the eve of the feast of Our Lady, Earl Gilbert de Clare left his Chamber of Shadows, slipped on the stairs and broke his neck. Was it an accident, or was he pushed down those steps?'

'Who would do that?'

'Why, Constable Hinkley, the Lady Joanna or Sir Ralph.'

'But the Lady Joanna was in her own chamber, the one you've just visited.'

'You are sure of that?'

'Oh yes. When the news was heard — '

'How did you hear it?'

'Sir Ralph found the body. He raised the alarm.'

'What was Sir Ralph doing in the east tower? The earl died around nine o'clock in the evening. Why wasn't Sir Ralph in his own quarters?'

'Earl Gilbert had planned to lead a great hunt the following morning. He intended to pursue the stag from dawn to dusk, as he put it.' Hinkley began to relax, sure of his story. 'Sir Ralph's duty was to prepare the hunt and he was to report to Earl Gilbert before he retired for the night.'

'Ah, so Sir Ralph went along and found his master lying at the bottom of the steps with his neck broken?' I paused, fingers to my lips, as if lost in deep thought. As my lecturer in theology at Oxford used to say, silence is more eloquent than any question. It sets your opponent's mind dancing as he wonders what trap you may be setting. Poor Hinkley, God bless him, grew more nervous.

'Why is Earl Gilbert's private room called the Chamber of Shadows?' I asked.

Hinkley looked away. 'You have to visit it, Master Henry,' he replied uncomfortably. 'It is octagonal in shape, specially constructed by the Earl.'

'Octagonal? Why should Earl Gilbert de Clare want an eight-sided chamber?'

Hinkley's Adam's apple bobbed like a leaf on a mill pond. 'The Earl Gilbert was a good lord,' he replied slowly. 'Sometimes he could be violent with his boot or whip but he paid wages on time and his servants and retinue were always well clothed and warm fed. He could be gracious and kind . . . '

'Except?'

'Except in his cups. Master Henry, I don't wish to speak ill of the dead but when he drank, the Earl became a different man, sometimes hot-tempered and choleric, at other times cold and hard, his eyes like daggers, his lips thin, as if he trusted no one. He could cut with his tongue and wound with his whip or his fists.'

'And the Chamber of Shadows?'

'It's what the servants called it.'

'Come, come, Master Matthew.' I smiled. 'I know the folklore. They say a demon can't lurk in an eight-sided chamber. Why was Earl Gilbert, the King's premier general, so frightened of the devil? Mass is said here, is it not? The castle is well stocked with crucifixes and holy water and Ricaud the priest must be ever ready to bless whatever you ask?'

Hinkley wiped his sweaty palms along his robe. 'There are demons and there are demons,' he whispered. 'I am not talking about the goblins and sprites who inhabit the woods.' He tapped a finger against his forehead. 'Earl Gilbert's demons lived here.'

'What demons?'

'Earl Gilbert did not find joy in his wife, only in wine, and when he drank deeply he howled like a trapped wolf.'

'Did he confide in the Lady Joanna?'

Hinkley shrugged one shoulder. 'They lived as lord and lady but I wonder whether they were man and wife. They must have been once, they have three children.'

'Where are they?'

'With the King at Westminster.'

'How was the Lady Joanna as a mother?'

'As she was to all of us, gracious and kind but distant. It was as if there was some invisible veil between her and the rest of the world, except where Sir Ralph was concerned.'

I stared at him.

Hinkley shook his head. 'I know nothing of their relationship. But when Sir Ralph was near her, Lady Joanna came to life. Something thawed inside her. She became flushed, eyes sparkling, lips always smiling. More like a young girl than a lady of the castle. But I swear I never saw them do anything untoward.'

I rested my elbows on my knees, stretching out both hands. 'So, we have a lord who has demons, drinks deeply and becomes vicious. His wife who acts like some lady of the snows, except where Sir Ralph is concerned. When did Monthermer enter the Earl's household?'

Hinkley closed his eyes. 'Earl Gilbert died in December the year before last. The previous February he had returned from the King's war in Wales. He should have come sooner but the snows were heavy and the roads were impassable. Lady Joanna was here with the children. Earl Gilbert rode into the courtyard, covered in mud but pleased to be back at Tonbridge. Lady Joanna went down. Yes, yes, that's right, she went down. I followed, as did Ricaud the priest, Tibault the seneschal and Lady Joanna's maid Alicia.'

'Is Alicia still here?'

'Oh yes, the King gave instructions that no one was to accompany his daughter into imprisonment.'

'And has she been questioned?'

'By Ricaud and Tibault though they carry no warrant. She expects to be questioned by you.'

'And she expects right,' I replied. 'But continue.'

'I remember the Lady Joanna took out a

cup of posset, its steam rose like incense from a censer. She was wearing gloves and carried the large cup in a velvet cloth. Sir Gilbert took it, drank deeply then handed it back. He swung down from the saddle and kissed her on each cheek. There were the usual greetings, some tears — Earl Gilbert had lost three men — and then he called along the line: 'Monthermer, you rascal, come here!' I saw the man dismount, swathed in a military cloak. He pulled back the hood and I was conscious of hair as black as a raven's, a rather narrow face but handsome, bright eyes and merry mouth. He walked with a swagger.'

'Did Earl Gilbert like him?'

'Oh yes, Monthermer was his favourite, you could see that. Sir Gilbert clapped him on the shoulder. 'My lady,' he said, 'let me introduce Ralph Monthermer, son of a boon companion of mine, now my personal squire. He has sworn on oath to be my man in peace and war.' '

'And the Lady Joanna?'

'God be my witness, Master Henry, she went pale. You know how she looks, hair like wheat on a summer's day but olive-skinned, like her mother, not pale.'

'You're sure about this?'

'I was standing next to her. It was as if

44

someone had picked up a piece of snow and pressed it against her hot neck. She blinked with shock and gawped like a maid.'

'And Monthermer?'

'He took her hand, kissed her fingertips and that was that.'

'So that was the beginning, was it?'

Hinkley nodded. 'Eventually others detected it as well. Monthermer was the perfect squire, a fine swordsman, a good body servant, witty and generous. In the great hall Lady Joanna's eyes would always search him out. Then one day I saw Monthermer glance back, soft-eyed, like a priest before a statue of the Virgin. He winked and the Lady Joanna, well, that's when I knew something was happening. Her face became transformed.' He wetted his lips. 'Heaven be my witness, I've never seen a woman smile like she did and I am almost fifty years of age. Have you ever seen someone smile with their whole body, Master Henry? It was as if her soul leaped out through her eyes. Then it was gone like a flash of sunlight.'

'And others came to know?'

'Oh yes. You can hide hate, malice . . . '

'You are quite the philosopher, Master Matthew.'

'I was a student in the Halls of Cambridge,' he smiled, 'till a company of royal archers came swaggering through the streets and I left learning and leisure for war and glory.'

'Go on with your story.'

'It was the best kept secret in Tonbridge though nothing untoward happened. After all, in many castles the lady is revered by her lord's knights.'

'And Earl Gilbert, did he notice?'

'If he did, he took no steps to stop it. I once overheard him sneer, 'If my wife needs a dog or a monkey to keep her happy, or a gallant, let her have it.' He was in his cups at the time.'

'Were Monthermer and the Lady Joanna often alone together?'

'Not that I saw. Oh, they danced the steps at Yuletide, their fingers kissed when Lady Joanna entered the chapel and Sir Ralph offered her holy water, but nothing more. No, it was the change in Lady Joanna that everyone noticed. She became alive, she would laugh, I mean really laugh not just a polite smile behind her fingers. She played more games with the children. She became busy round the castle. If Earl Gilbert went hunting, Lady Joanna joined him and Monthermer was always there. He often escorted her down to see her confessor, Father Benedict, at the village church. Sometimes I comforted myself that it was more like the love between a sister and brother but, if the truth be known, I think she adored him.'

'And he her?'

'Oh yes, but in a chivalrous way.'

Was Hinkley telling the truth? I wondered. Had he heeded my warning in the hall and decided to give his version before Ricaud and Tibault cut at these two lovers with their sour tongues.

'Why,' I asked, 'did the Lady Joanna, the King's daughter, a countess, a landowner, a great beauty like her mother, love a simple knight? I called you a philosopher, Master Matthew. Why do you think she loved Monthermer?'

Hinkley got to his feet. I realised that whatever the truth of what he had said before, now he would speak his mind openly and honestly. He walked to the far wall and back before he spoke.

'For two reasons, Master Henry, and in this matter the fact that the Lady Joanna is the King's daughter is of no account. We all have a hunger to be loved and to love, and the Lady Joanna is no exception. She has a real appetite for loving, which Earl Gilbert only sharpened; he never satisfied it. By some trick of fate Monthermer filled the terrible emptiness in Lady Joanna's soul.

47

Monthermer is a soldier but he is charming, gentle, good with the children, not only the Earl's but others of the castle. He laughs easily, forgives quickly. There is something about him . . . ' Hinkley hesitated.

'What?' I prompted.

'Young Monthermer reminded me of the King in his youth — generous to a fault. It was no wonder Earl Gilbert liked him.'

'But the Earl's liking must have faltered. If there's one thing worse than seeing someone paying court to your wife, it's seeing your wife lead the chase.'

'Ah, but not Earl Gilbert.' Hinkley sucked on his teeth. 'Earl Gilbert didn't seem to care.'

'You are sure of that?'

Hinkley sat down very close as if he didn't want me to miss his next words.

'It was stronger than that,' he hissed. 'It was as if Earl Gilbert wanted Sir Ralph to become his wife's lover.'

'Surely not,' I retorted. 'No man plays the pimp for his own wife.'

'I can only tell you what I saw. Earl Gilbert left them together time and again. Moreover, when the King came to Tonbridge, it was Earl Gilbert, not the Lady Joanna as is generally believed, who insisted that Monthermer be dubbed a knight. To his dying day, Earl

Gilbert did not falter in his affection for Monthermer.'

Hinkley was telling the truth. Did not Your Grace say the same to me at Westminster? I asked if there had been any whisper of scandal, if Sir Gilbert had ever laid accusation against Monthermer, and you replied no, the Red Earl had nothing but praise for this Welsh squire.

I looked at Hinkley. 'Did Earl Gilbert's fancy wander?'

Hinkley leaned back. 'A serving wench, Maude, said that Earl Gilbert might ride a horse but he could not hold a lance.'

'Was he impotent?'

'That's what the wench said. She claimed the Earl fumbled her in the wine cellar.'

'And where is she now?'

'Gone, I believe.'

I got to my feet. 'And so must I be.' I smiled down at Hinkley. 'At least to bed. But first, let me see Earl Gilbert's bedchamber.'

'It's sealed. The King's men put their wax on the door.'

'And I have the power to break those seals. Come.'

Earl Gilbert's bedchamber stood at the end of the gallery; there were two rooms between his and that of his wife. It was small, dusty, the smell rather fetid. Hinkley lit some candles and opened the shutters. The bed was a four-poster, the curtains of dark murrey drawn close. The walls were half covered by wooden panelling, above which hung pictures and a crucifix. An aumbrie, chest and coffers were the only furniture. Despite Hinkley's protests, I went through them but found nothing untoward. There were three books chained to a shelf. Their contents surprised me. You know the type, Your Grace, bought from the parchment-sellers in Oxford and Cambridge or on the scriveners' stalls at St Paul's: works on witchcraft and dreams. There was no trace of his wife, no keepsake, not a scrap.

On a table beside the bed was a small, jewel-encrusted psalter, its pages stiff and gold-edged. On the folios at the back, where people write their own prayers, Earl Gilbert had scrawled time and again: '*Miserere Domine, miserere mei*: have mercy on me, O Lord, have mercy on me.' And other snatches from the Psalms, including: 'My sins are always before me. Blot out my offence.'

I put the psalter down. What had the Earl done in his life to demand such mercy? I was about to move away when I noticed a small bowl containing two pieces of velvet wrapped round something hard.

50

'Earplugs,' I remarked. 'When the Earl slept he placed these in his ears.'

'He also wore a velvet eye band.'

I sat down on the bed and stared up at Hinkley. 'Did the Earl not sleep well?'

Hinkley looked uneasy. 'He claimed he was haunted. He saw ghosts and sprites. Ask Tibault the seneschal. Guards were always placed near his chamber.'

Hinkley then left and I returned to my own room to pen this letter.

As Your Grace can see, my inquiries so far raise many questions but supply very few answers.

Written at Tonbridge, the feast of St Ancclebus, April 1297.

Letter 3

To Joanna, Princess of England and queen of my heart, Ralph Monthermer, her beloved captive, sends his fealty and total devotion.

They say to love is to be brushed by the hand of God. I give thanks every moment of the day that I am so favoured. The candles guttered as I deciphered your letter. I cannot say whether the seal was broken and someone else tried to read your loving messages. What do I care? Even before I began, I could sense your passion. I held your letter to my cheek as I wish to God I could hold your hand. It is so hard to endure this winter of the spirit and I wait for your love like a beggar at the door of a church. The merest scrap is a banquet.

My time with you had become like a dream, half lost in sleep, but your letter brought it to life again. I was like a falcon that had been released, wings spread, flying to the sun. Outside my window wild roses grow. I stretched out and pulled one in, white and soft, still covered with the morning dew. I kissed it and whispered words of endearment which the breeze, as well as the force of my passion, will convey to you. Soul sings to soul. Even without letters or messengers, you know that I love you.

Like you, I was taken by force and stealth, and I am imprisoned in a chamber just above a small orchard at Bristol Castle. But so far your father's treatment of me has been honourable. 'You are to be well treated,' Sir Miles Sempringham, the Constable, declared on my arrival. 'You will be given good victuals, a clean chamber, books, a change of linen and clothing.' And he has been true to his word.

Sir Miles is an old warhorse. He claims to have served with my father against the Welsh and he often visits me to recount old battles and daring feats of arms. The castle is well guarded by men-at-arms and archers. No one can approach my tower without a special pass. I understand your messenger was kindly received; Sir Miles brought your letter to me personally. Nonetheless, I am not taken by his bluff ways. He is of your father's school, a hale and hearty warrior but with a mind as sharp as a knife. You can achieve more by kindness than cruelty seems the path Sir Miles treads. He has told me that he is closely advised by one of your father's men, a clerk of the Royal Chapel, Henry Trokelowe, but as yet I have not met him.

My days are spent waiting, thinking and reflecting. My only true terror is that I may not see your face again. I am a soldier, more used to the camp than the silken courtesies of the court. Two demons afflict me. First, that I may be ambushed by death crawling like an assassin from a sewer and my eyes will never again mirror yours. If that happens, remember this. I shall wait for you by the gates of eternity. The second is my confinement, my absence from you. If I cannot have you then what use is life? I have read your letter time and again. I know every phrase. I could recite it like a troubadour does a song. I have taken it apart, piece by piece, searching for hidden meanings. I understand your fear. Our secret is safe. No flattery, no kindness, no terror will draw it from me.

I do not know what will happen. Sir Miles has told me that the King's temper has not cooled but worsens by the day.

'You are a commoner, Sir Ralph,' he declared.

'I am a knight,' I replied.

'Aye, sir, but dubbed at the Lady Joanna's request.' Sir Miles sat on the table looking down at me. 'You were a squire in Earl Gilbert's retinue. How dare you woo the Lady Joanna, a royal widow, the King's daughter? What right did you have?'

I could not answer.

'Well, sir?'

'Love,' I replied. 'I love the Lady Joanna.'

He shook his head. 'You're too young to remember the King's wife, Eleanor of Castile.' He smiled to himself. 'Skin of gold, she had, and her hair shone like the sun. Her eyes were ice-blue. A vision of beauty, Sir Ralph. Her very smile made the heart dance and the blood sing. I loved her,' he continued, 'as did all the King's knights, but we knew our place. You should know yours.'

Time and again the old warrior would return to sing the same song to a different tune. I have no doubt that Sir Miles's questions were put on the King's behalf. Did I love you for gain? Did I think that, through you, I would achieve easy access to the King's favour, to lands and titles? Sir Miles was not so blunt but his purpose was clear. He was most circumspect. He never talked of intimate matters; he did not ask whether I had lain with you or what the true nature of our friendship and love was. And there was something else. I caught it in his eyes, an unspoken accusation. I felt afraid. Do they know of our secret already? Could someone at the castle have betrayed us? But who knew? Only the priest and the other, both of whom are loyal and have been sworn to secrecy.

My chamber is large. Only recently have I realised that high in the wall is a squint hole where someone listens. Your father? A member of the court? Some snivelling clerk taking down everything I say to Sir Miles? My mood changed. I became like a soldier walking through a forest, fearing an ambush, an arrow from the dark. I discovered the peephole when Sir Miles returned. He sat down and I leaned against the door.

'Why do you visit me here, Sir Miles?' I asked.

The bluff blue eyes shifted a little. 'To see that you are well.'

'No, Sir Miles, it's more than that. I may, as you say, be common born but God gave me wits. There's something else.

Sir Miles shook his head and got to his feet. He walked towards the door. I had to stand aside but I gripped him by the wrist.

'Tell me, what is it you want?' I insisted.

Sir Miles's eyes moved to the squint hole in the wall — that's what alerted me to it. He freed his hand and grasped me round the neck, pulling my head close.

'Did you love Earl Gilbert as much as you do his widow?'

I stood back. He put a finger to his lips and, before I could reply, he had gone. He has not returned, at least not by himself. Now, when he visits me, one of his retinue is always present — a physician or a priest or the captain of the guard. My fear still remains. What else are they searching for? Our secret? But how would they know of it? And what did Sir Miles mean when he asked if I loved Earl Gilbert?

When I was first taken I thought I had been betrayed. On reading your letter, I now know you did what you promised: to be honest with your father, tell him the secrets of your heart and leave the rest to God. Nevertheless, Sir Miles's question haunts me. I am reminded of what happened when I was first arrested, though I heed your warning that we must be prudent in what we write. No doubt they permit us to communicate by letter in order to find out more. Your father's clerks are skilled, they may well break the cipher we use. Did you, my love, destroy the other letters? Or were they seized? Your father's visit to Tonbridge was carefully timed to take place in that shadowy period between winter and spring when the paths and tracks are clogged with mud and few people go visiting. I, of course, was absent. It was all planned from the very start. That day at Wallingford meant more to your father than it did to us. Like innocents we dreamed on, unaware of the lengthening shadows. Do you remember how pleased I was when I received my commission to take a force north to the Scottish march under Lord Neville? I thought it was a mark of your father's trust. In truth, I was being despatched out of the way. I left Tonbridge in such high hopes, with your glove inside my jerkin. At least six times a day I would take it out and smell your perfume. I'd close my eyes and pretend that you were near to me.

The weather was cold and hard on the march. We were at Mytton in the Yorkshire Dales when your father struck. I had taken a group of horsemen out. On my return I was summoned to Lord Neville's tent.

'Come in, come in, Ralph!' he called.

I stepped inside. Only then did I see the guards. They closed about me. John Berkeley, Neville's captain, drew both his sword and his dagger from his belt.

'What mischief is this?' I cried.

Neville sat down, no smile on his face now. He sipped from his cup and moved the candle so the dancing shadows hid his face.

'Sir Ralph Monthermer,' he declared gruffly, 'you are under arrest. Master Berkeley here is charged to take you to Bristol Castle and confine you at the King's pleasure.'

I would have leaped forward but Berkeley held me fast.

'For the love of God,' I shouted. 'Is this a jest?'

'No jest,' responded Lord Neville grimly.

'I am a knight,' I protested. 'I hold a royal commission.'

'And I hold the King's warrant!' Neville retorted. He picked it up from the table. I glimpsed the seal. 'Sir Ralph Monthermer, you are under arrest for treason!'

Oh, heart of my hearts, I went cold. Did they know? Had they found out?

'What treason?' I asked. 'I am the King's most loyal servant.'

'Aye, and if the truth be known, also the Lady Joanna's, the widowed Countess of Gloucester, a princess of the blood!' I saw the envy in Neville's eyes. 'You, sir, are a common knight and you have paid court to the King's own daughter during her time of widowhood. I fought alongside the Earl Gilbert.' Neville rose, came forward and pushed his face close to mine. 'What right do you have even to look at her? A mere squire, a base-born — '

I lashed out. I could take no more. Berkeley had relaxed his grip. I caught

59

Neville in his sneering face and turned on my would-be captors. Berkeley, a sergeant-at-arms with more brawn than brain, was confused. I was through the tent flap before he even knew I was gone. God knows I should not have done it but I had only one thought and it will make you smile. I was in the wilds of Yorkshire yet I believed I could return to you.

I ran through the camp, scattering men grouped around their fires. A groom was taking a horse down to the lines; I knocked him aside and then I rode like the wind. To them it must have looked like flight, but I had to see you again. I had to tell my heart of hearts that, whatever happened, I'd remain constant and true.

God bless the horse's strong heart; in our flight he showed more sense than I did. I broke free of the camp and sped through the trees along a forest pathway. The freezing air chilled my sweat-soaked face. I reined in. I did not know where I was or what direction to take. I looked over my shoulder and heard the sound of pursuit.

Plucking sword and dagger from their sheaths, I stood with my back to a tree, prepared to take allcomers. My pursuers arrived and dismounted. Some were carrying torches. They fanned out. One, young and inexperienced, came running forward, eager to make his mark. Instead he received one. He backed off, clutching the cut high in his arm. Berkeley led the rest at a half-crouch. For a while the grizzled sergeant-at-arms studied me closely, watching my eyes, the way I stood, then he edged forward, his hand lifted in the sign of peace.

'The reputation and valour of Sir Ralph Monthermer are well known,' he said. 'Yet I swear we mean you no harm. My orders are to take you back alive.' He edged forward. 'For God's sake, lad,' he whispered hoarsely, 'look around you!'

I didn't shift my gaze.

He straightened. 'I mean no trick. Look around you, sir. Do you want to die here? Where there's life there's always hope.'

'I have your word?' I said.

'You are a knight,' he replied. 'If I took your life I would have to answer for it to the King.' Berkeley's hand came forward. 'Your sword, sir.'

I passed it over. His men raced forward but Berkeley growled at them. They did not bind my hands but I was made to share a horse with one of the archers and taken back to camp. Neville's mouth was bleeding but he'd regained his wits and offered no further insult. Two days later Berkeley and a group of archers took me south. In a village church I swore an oath I would not try to escape.

'Just till we get to Bristol, lad,' Berkeley smiled. 'If you escape, the King will have my head.'

I kept my oath, as he had kept his. Nine days later we entered Bristol Castle. Berkeley shook my hand, wished me well and handed me over to the Constable.

So I became the guest of Sir Miles Sempringham. He, too, wanted me to take an oath that I would not escape but I refused. Instead I insisted that whatever charges were levelled against me be published in open court or, because I am a knight, be permitted to purge myself in trial by battle. Yesterday evening I repeated my demand for satisfaction.

'Satisfaction from whom, Sir Ralph?' asked Sir Miles.

'From the person who has caused my imprisonment.'

Sir Miles pointed to my shadow on the wall. 'In that case you had better seek satisfaction from that. You are the cause.'

'Because I dared to love?'

'No, Sir Ralph, because you aimed too high. King's daughters are not for the likes of you or me.'

'Is that all?' I said. 'Because Joanna

Plantagenet happens to be the daughter of the King of England?'

He would not answer and left me. I felt fury raging. I took a piece of straw from the floor, pretended it was a sword and, following Sir Miles's advice, fought my shadow till my body ran with sweat. I heard a sound from the spyhole high in the wall.

'Go hang yourself!' I shouted then lay on the bed and thought of you.

I wish I could remember the first time we met. Oh, I know where it was and when but I want to recall every detail. Where the clouds were in the sky. What was underfoot. I want to recall your first look and, above all, your first touch: whether it was day, noon or night, sunshine or rain, cold or dry. I now realise I loved you before I saw your face or knew your name. You are the birthday of my life. We were born together and, if necessary, we will die together. When our bodies are scattered dust, our souls will fly like eagles on the winds of heaven.

I jumped from my bed and stared up at the spyhole.

'Tell the King,' I shouted, 'I am his most loyal servant but the Lady Joanna is my first love. Tell the King I will love his daughter until the rocks melt and the seas run dry!'

No sound, no reply. I lay down and

watched the daylight fade. At such times I tell myself how, on the other side of the darkness, your heart beats like mine, your thoughts are with me. Oh, lady of my soul, spring is now here. The wild roses that climb up the walls of the castle are just within reach outside my window. Every day, at dawn and dusk, I lean out and whisper to them. I pray that God in his goodness will take my message to you.

I have your letter close. I do not care about Master Henry Trokelowe or spies who might break our cipher. As for our secret, let Hell freeze over before my tongue speaks what my heart knows. Nevertheless, I am concerned. Oh, I understand the King's wrath. I know how all his children are mere pawns upon a royal chessboard. The Princess Eleanor is to be sent abroad, your brother is affianced to this or that princess to further the great Edward's dreams of dominating Europe. But what other matter fuels the King's anger?

Sometimes I become frightened, not of death, only of losing you, of an accident, something which could be explained away. It nearly happened. After a week of imprisonment and being watched from that spyhole, I was allowed out into the tilt yard to exercise with the castle garrison. No one really took much notice of me. I was given a wooden sword and shield; like the rest I danced and spun, letting my blows release the pent-up fury of my heart. On such occasions a blood-red haze can cloud the fighter's mind. I came up against a swordsman. At first I didn't really care who it was. I glimpsed dark eyes and a grizzled face almost hidden by the broad nose guard and conical helmet. I gave him a blow upon his shoulder and he stood back.

'Why, Sir Ralph, you lay on hard.'

'I am a swordsman,' I replied.

My opponent looked at the wooden stick he carried and threw it to the ground.

'A child's plaything!' he scoffed.

All my rage was upon me. Perhaps it was the sneering look in his eyes, or the way he turned to smile at his companions who now formed a ring around him.

'Playthings are for children!' I retorted. 'What else do you expect?'

'That's an insult, Bastogne,' someone shouted.

My opponent looked at me, lower lip jutting as he considered the worth of the insult. I studied him more closely. He was tall, thickset with the long arms of a born swordsman. I recalled the skill he had displayed.

He stepped forward and tapped me gently on the tip of my nose, which provoked a ripple of laughter from his companions. 'If you wish, Sir Ralph, we can, as St Paul says, put away childish things.'

I accepted the challenge.

Shield and sword were provided and Bastogne squared up. Only then did I feel a shiver of fear. I glanced around. No sign of Sempringham or any of his officers. Bastogne had the style and poise of a professional fighting man, a mercenary.

We struck and parried. We closed and drew apart. The tilt yard fell silent except for the scrape of steel. God knows, my beloved, I am arrogant and pride does indeed come before a fall. Bastogne was a superb swordsman. Do you remember how we two once fenced with wooden canes in the woods near Tonbridge? You asked me why I kept staring at you. I replied that swordsmen always watch the eyes, not the hands, though as regards your eyes, it was a pleasure rather than a duty. I can see them now, brimming with laughter as you lashed out with that cane. I prodded you in the stomach, you pretended to be mortally wounded and fell to the ground. In those opening parries with Bastogne I recalled you but, this time, your eyes weren't smiling. It was as if your soul had come to warn me. Bastogne's eyes betrayed him. This was no mock fight. This man intended to take my life. Backwards and forwards we parried, cut and clashed. We locked sword arms and he searched for his knife. I pushed him away and we set to again. Then Sir Miles appeared. He shouted at Bastogne, came between us and ordered me back to my cell.

I was covered in sweat and dust. Sempringham had a wooden tub filled with hot water brought to my cell. I remembered the spyhole high in the wall and, not from modesty but, pricked by suspicion, I kept my body covered. At one time I crouched down and, taking some mud from my boot, rubbed it in as if it was a scar along my stomach then turned very quickly for the spy to have a glimpse of me. I crouched in the tub and washed myself. I felt like a foolish maid yet I couldn't understand Sir Miles's kindness. The bath houses are near the tilt yard. I have washed there before; the weather was balmy and warm so why have a tub brought specially up?

After I had dressed, I sat on the bed while Sir Miles brought in servants to remove the tub.

'Was it your idea, Sir Miles?' I asked.

He coloured slightly. 'The bath tub was brought up as a courtesy.'

'I wasn't talking about the bath tub,' I

replied, 'but the fight down there in the yard.' I got to my feet and faced him squarely. 'On your word as a knight, was Bastogne under orders to kill me?'

'Don't be stupid!'

I held his gaze and noted his discomfort.

'Bastogne was not to kill you,' he whispered. 'He was to give you a cut, as a warning and to trim your feathers lest you fly. It will not happen again.' Then he pulled back the door and was gone.

Later that day, just as dusk fell and the guards brought my evening meal, a black-garbed, balding, sharp-nosed individual was escorted into my cell. I could tell from Sir Miles's face he wasn't happy with this new arrival.

'Sir Ralph,' he said, 'this is Master Eustace Cordell, a public notary attached to the city council of Bristol. He is indentured by the King to supervise royal rights in the city.'

I shook the man's sweaty, limp hand and took an instant dislike to him. It wasn't just his bloodless lips, cracked teeth and sharp, furtive eyes but the way he assessed me as he would a sack of wool. He sat prim as a maid on the three-legged stool and waved me back to the bed as if he didn't wish me to approach too close.

'You are?' he asked in a nasal voice.

'You know who I am,' I retorted. 'Otherwise you wouldn't be here!'

The man sniggered but the eyes never changed.

'You are Sir Ralph Monthermer,' he continued, 'the son of Edmund and Agnes Monthermer who own manors and lands outside Abergavenny in Wales. You are related to the powerful Mortimer family. In the campaign of the year twelve hundred and ninety-four to ninety-five you brought yourself to the attention of Sir Gilbert de Clare, the Red Earl of Gloucester. I am here to ask you some preliminary questions and I shall be returning tomorrow to continue.'

This strange fellow then unrolled the scroll of parchment on his lap.

'Are you an Adamite?'

'No!' I replied sharply.

'But you know who they are?'

'Of course.'

'Have you ever been married?'

'No.'

After more such foolish questions — do I have children, do I attend Mass, when was I last at confession — Cordell stood up, bowed towards me and left the cell, Sir Miles behind him.

If Bastogne's swordplay worried me, Cordell's questions started a thousand and one hares coursing. What does your father intend? What trickery is being planned?

Sir Miles returned. He was shamefaced but he brought a fresh jug of wine and said that if I wished to reply to your letter, a messenger would be leaving just before dawn.

Darkness falls, I must bring this to an end. So, what can I say? You talk of constancy. Hold up your hand, my beloved, look at the veins and remember, as long as blood flows and heart beats, I love you.

Written at Bristol on the feast of St Florian, May 1297.

Letter 4

From Joanna, Princess of England, to her own true heart, Ralph Monthermer, health and greetings.

The night before your letter came, my mind wandered in that mad, tormented valley of misbegotten dreams where fear strikes like a deadly snake and a swooping, unnamed terror looses legions of sinister ghosts. Unresolved fears from the past, and for the future, came crowding round me. I woke sweat-soaked. I thought I heard a raven croak outside my window then a distant kennel-tied dog hurled raucous abuse at the stars.

I threw the coverlet back and pressed my hot feet against the cold, wooden floor. I ran across, opened the small casement window and glimpsed the trees: dark oak, paler ash, the curling yew tree, the grey willow, white poplars, all moon-washed silver. In my conceit, as well as hope, I thought you might be sheltering there. Only dreams! The convent lay silent, the occasional light flickered from some outhouse, kitchen or scullery where the lay nuns worked, preparing suitable refreshment for the sisters after they have sung their early office. I was invited to join them but when I am in church, the only God I think of is you. May the Lord forgive me!

I wrapped a cloak round me, took a tinder and lit a candle. I sat down at my table and scratched a poem, my own matins to you. I cannot bear this separation; the loneliness is so crushing, I could throw my head back and howl like that dog but what good would it do?

My poem is not a troubadour song or a minstrel's jingle but a prayer to God for forgiveness and for his help. You are my world. What else can I do, except write? Touch and sight are forbidden, but we are united in soul and that soothes some of my pain.

I did not know I could write so quickly. The Lady Abbess has been most generous. In my own large chamber stands a small chancery desk well furnished with ink, vellum, quills and sealing wax. I meant to write a letter but, on the breeze, came the first sounds of the sisters singing prime, their dawn hymn to Christ the Lord, so I composed my poem. I crossed out certain lines and began to write again. Snatches of the Psalms disturbed my spiritual exercise:

Are you asleep, O God?
Why do you not wake and rise?
Bare your arm!
Show mercy and justice
To this your poor servant.

Isn't it strange? For the first time in my
life those Psalms, which always seemed as
dry and dull as dust, took on a life and
vibrancy of their own. I became guilty.
Should I not love God as I love you?
But then I took comfort from the words
of Christ: 'Much shall be forgiven her for
much she has loved.'

This is my poem; this is my hymn. Every
soul has its song and this is mine, a prayer
for forgiveness, a deep desire that God, who
is love itself, will not allow my love for you
to be frustrated.

I slip from heaven's golden court.
                Kyrie Eleison.
And plunge like Lucifer
Through the darkest void.
                Kyrie Eleison.
Around me, scarlet in
The heavens, flow rivers of Grace.
                Kyrie Eleison.
The cross of Christ, etched
In the fabric of things, calls out.

Christe Eleison.
But its voice, shrieking
In Love's own agony,
I ignore.
Christe Eleison.
Those who ignore the
Cross are crucified themselves.
Christe Eleison.
With no resurrection, no
Sunday morn, shot through with life.
Christe Eleison.
Like an arrow, the soul
Plunges into its own dark caverns.
Kyrie Eleison.
Lost, till the hunter of
Souls and the heart's own searcher,
Follows it down.
Kyrie Eleison.
And, like the gentlest dove,
Caught on the wing,
Takes the arrow to itself.

After I had finished my psalm, I sat half listening to the chanting from the convent church. My mind travelled back to our castle chapel at Tonbridge on that fateful Candlemas Eve. Father was sitting on the altar steps, I on a small stool beside him. He was tapping his foot on the ground, a sign that he was impatient at having to choose his words carefully.

'What is it, Father?' I asked.

He smiled boyishly. Oh, he knows how to pluck at the strings of my heart! No longer the King, the mighty warrior, the great armoured knight on his black warhorse waging war against the Welsh and Scots. Isn't it strange the tricks parents play? They become the child and you become the adult.

My father stretched out his great hand, squeezed my fingers and began to sing beneath his breath: 'Oh, my love is like a flower in bloom, yet the bloom goes. The flower dies but the memory of it grows stronger.'

He was thinking of Eleanor. I suspect he always thinks of her. The day she died, he grew old and something died in him. I remember him telling me the news in the manor hall at King's Langley.

'She's dead, Joanna,' he gasped. The tears streamed down his face yet he never made a sound. I have never seen anyone weep like he did.

'She's dead, Joanna. I miss her so!'

In his grief I forgot mine.

'She shouldn't have died,' he whispered. 'It was only a slight fever. Nothing important. I'll hang the physicians. I'll hang each and every one of them. I'll fill all the gallows round London!'

Of course he never did. He brought Mother's body back to Westminster like a priest carries the sacrament. At every place where the coffin and cortège paused, he built a memorial to her name, including the last resting place, the 'Cross of the Dear Queen', here in London. I have seen it ablaze with candles, even now, years later.

He confided in me then and on that Candlemas Eve he was about to confide again, only this time he loosed a host of terrors into our lives.

'What is it, Father?' I raised his hand and kissed the knuckles.

He scratched his cheek and shuffled his feet. 'I am to marry again,' he declared harshly.

I dropped his hand. I could not believe it. How could a man who had loved so deeply marry again? But we make mistakes, don't we? The cruellest fault is that we believe that others, especially those who are of the same flesh and blood, think like ourselves.

'I am to marry again, Joanna,' he repeated. He looked at me, eyes hard. 'The war with France has forced my hand.' The southern ports were thick with troops and every cog from the mouth of the Thames to the Scottish border had been assembled in a great fleet, ready to carry fire and sword into northern France. 'There will be no war,' he said. 'The Pope has intervened. Old, fat Boniface!'

'Then we should rejoice, Father.'

'I cannot afford a war,' he muttered. 'The Scots are in rebellion and Philip of France no longer bluffs. This time his troops will cross into Gascony. If they do, we'll lose. So I've decided on a treaty. There will be peace and the women and children of England will rejoice. I'll keep Gascony. Philip will not interfere in Scotland and we'll have discussions. We'll talk and we'll talk and let our lawyers loose to talk again. In return,' he clapped his hands gently, 'the Pope has proposed that the two royal families of France and England be doubly united. I am to marry Margaret, Philip IV's sister. My only son and heir is to be betrothed to Philip's daughter Isabella.'

'Have you met the lady?' I asked.

He shook his head. 'No. They say she is fair and gracious, with a comely body and pleasant wit.'

'Will you love her?'

'You only love once, Joanna,' he said. 'God is very firm on that. You get one chance and that is all. I had my opportunity. Now I must marry for reasons of state, to keep the peace, to be depicted in the courts of Europe as a prince who loves justice more than war.'

Oh God, Ralph, that is when I made my mistake. Crafty Father, sly as Reynard! He could outfox a fox. Do you remember the moves I taught you when we played chess? You force your opponent to think a certain move is important but it is the next one that traps him. Father did that.

'Are you pleased, Joanna?'

'I am pleased for you, Father. It is not good for a man to live alone.'

'Do you believe that?' he asked abruptly. 'Do you believe we only get one chance of love? Here we are, father and daughter, both widowed.' He glimpsed the pain in my eyes and grasped my hand. 'Was Earl Gilbert a good husband? You have three children.'

'Why do you ask, Father?'

'I've heard stories.' His gaze refused to meet mine. 'Just rumours and gossip.'

I ignored the slight chill of fear that raised the hairs on the back of my neck. The candle flames danced and I wondered if my husband's ghost was standing in the shadows of that silent chapel.

'Earl Gilbert was a strange man,' Father mused. 'He could be violent and merciless, I know. Never mind!' He let my fingers go.

'Do you believe we have one chance of love? Tell me, Joanna. Tell me that I have said right.'

'For you and Mother, yes, you have said right, Father.' I wetted my lips. 'But my — '

'Would you marry again?' Father interrupted. 'You have met Amadeus of Savoy, have you not? A powerful nobleman, a goodly man. He has the ear of princes and is a close friend of the Pope.'

Oh Ralph, my heart went cold. I became so tense I could not move, like a rabbit who sits in terror and watches the weasel approach.

'Father, I am a widow with three children.'

'To me, Joanna, you are still a young woman of twenty-five.'

I did not care about Amadeus of Savoy. Oh, I considered him fair enough but . . . I realised I was in a passageway, free of one dungeon only to be led to another.

'Joanna, what is the matter?'

'Father, you have been most fortunate,' I blurted out. 'You and Eleanor loved each other, you still love passionately, not even death has extinguished that flame.' I lifted my head and held his gaze, a gambler ready to stake all on one final throw. 'I did not love Earl Gilbert. I married him because I am your daughter and he was a powerful landowner, your premier general, a man you kept by your side by marrying him to me because you could not fully trust him. Now he is dead. I have done my duty, Father. Now I wish to follow my heart's desire. I did not love the Earl Gilbert. I will not love Amadeus of Savoy, or Philip of France, or Louis his son, or some Spanish prince or Italian count, or a great English earl. I love already.'

Father's face was suddenly that of a hawk sitting on its perch ready to strike. I recalled a phrase muttered by one of his clerks: 'The will of the King has force of law and the wrath of the King means death.'

'What do you mean, daughter?'

'I will tell you honestly, Sire. I love Sir Ralph Monthermer. I always have, I always will. I shall not marry anyone else.'

'Monthermer!' The name was spat out like a piece of gristle which had hurt his gums. 'That base-born Welsh squire!' My father sprang to his feet. 'You, Joanna, Princess of England! The stories are true! Is that why you had me knight him?'

'I did not ask you to knight him!' I, too, was on my feet, all caution forgotten. The prospect of another arranged marriage was like a cold shroud draped round my body. 'And what stories, Father? Since when have you set spies on your children?'

'I don't need to spy. The chatter is all over Westminster. You and Monthermer, dewy-eyed, playing cat's cradle with each other, whispering in window seats and galleries.' My father's face had turned pale with fury. 'And what about at night, eh? Soft footfalls in the gallery. Tapping on the door.'

'What are you implying, Father? That I am some strumpet from Cheapside? My love for Sir Ralph — '

'Oh, for Sir Ralph,' my father mimicked me.

'He's a brave warrior, Father, a good swordsman.'

'Aye, and a jouster,' the King snarled. 'Lance ever at the ready. No wonder he crowned you queen of the tournament!' His face was now only inches from mine. 'I saw it then. My heart couldn't believe what my eyes witnessed.' He breathed in noisily. 'And what do you expect me to do, daughter dear? Give way? Escort you into church so you and Sir Ralph can exchange vows? Have pennies and flowers thrown over you at the door? Perhaps afterwards I can create him Earl of Gloucester, or make him my heir. Even better, he could be King!'

'Father, you are being stupid and cruel.'

'No, I am being a pragmatist. You are, as

you have said, my daughter, my blood, my flesh, Countess of Gloucester, a royal widow, not some tavern wench or coy mistress. When you marry, you marry for reasons of state, for the furtherance of our family's glory and the peace of this kingdom.'

'Like you did, Father, with Mother?'

'I married her before I loved her.'

'Liar!' I screamed back. 'You loved her the moment you saw her, you know that. You loved her then, you love her now.'

Only then did the King's face soften. He sighed and slumped back down onto the steps. I thought his mood was changing. I should have known he was simply changing masks.

'You always were strong-willed, fearless and relentless in what you wanted.'

'Sire, I am your daughter.'

'Joanna, when you were a child you never wanted anything. It is what separated you from your brothers and sisters. Edward, well, you know Edward, with his tame lion and his greyhounds, his hawks and his falcons, his horses and God knows what else. Eleanor was vain. The psalmist must have thought of her when he wrote the line, 'Vanity of vanities and all is vanity.' Mary, she wanted to be a nun from the moment she could walk, so pious, so boring. But you, Joanna, were different. All you wanted was to be near your mother and myself. You'd hide away beneath the tables or behind the arras. Peek through keyholes.' He smiled. 'I asked you once what you wanted as a birthday present. Somebody had been telling you stories about Merlin. You must have been only about four. 'I want a magic cloak,' you replied, 'to make me invisible.' '

'Now, Father, I want Ralph Monthermer.'

The King wasn't listening. 'Squirrel, that's what I called you,' he murmured. 'My little squirrel, with those fat cheeks and unblinking eyes, the way you'd sit and watch.' He breathed in, nostrils flaring as he fought to control his temper. 'Joanna, you are Countess of Gloucester. It was a good marriage, wasn't it? You have three lovely children . . . '

I felt the rage boiling within me.

'Gilbert was a fine man,' he added, 'a brawny fighter.'

'What do you know?' I hissed. 'He was married before!'

Father blinked.

'Of course he was married before! The Pope annulled his marriage. Do you know why? Because his first wife was terrified of him!'

'No, no, no.' Edward waved a be-ringed hand.

'Tell me, Father, did you love de Clare who, thirty years ago, raised rebellion against you? Isn't it true, Father, you were frightened of him, just a little? So you thought you'd keep him sweet by giving him your daughter.'

'I wasn't frightened of de Clare.' The King spoke through gritted teeth. 'If he had taken the field I would have defeated him. Every marriage has its tensions but he treated you as a great lady and gave you three children.'

'He was a cold-hearted, demon-filled man!' The words were out before I could stop them.

The King's mouth gaped.

'He was cold and hard, and in his cups he would turn nasty. He kept the shadows of his soul hidden behind courtly etiquette and polite manners. But you did not see him drunk, did you, Father? The froth high on his lips, staggering across the bedchamber, a belt in one hand, a dagger in the other.'

'He would not have dared!'

'Oh, and what would you do, Father?' I asked in mock sweetness. 'Pass a law saying a man cannot beat his wife? God forgive me, Sire, I do have three lovely children. I hold their little bodies close to me and even now the tears scald my eyes although I know the manner of their conception is not their fault.'

Edward was watching me intently.

'I was raped. Do you understand that, Father? He took me just like soldiers take women in some captured town, brutally, without affection. Afterwards he would sleep like a pig, till the demons came and he would wake up screaming.'

'What demons?'

'God only knows.'

'I am sorry,' Father mumbled. 'Amadeus of Savoy is not like that.'

'I could not care if Amadeus is an angel sent by God. I shall not, I will not marry him!'

'Why, because of your lover?'

'He is not my lover.'

'Then what is he?'

'He is my knight.'

'What is this?' The King spread his hands. 'Some courtly romance? Some tale from King Arthur? Are you the Holy Grail? And Monthermer Sir Percival?'

'Do not mock me, Father.'

'I have sent Sir Ralph north to fight the Scots. Whether he comes back or not — '

I struck my father, full in the mouth. He sprang forward, hand going to his dagger.

'Go on!' I shouted. 'Draw it!' I ripped the neckline of my dress. 'Go on, Edward of England, strike once, strike deep!'

The King's dagger was in his hand. I drew the small poignard I kept in my belt.

I stepped closer. He did not flinch but watched my eyes.

'Here, in God's own house,' I vowed, 'I take this most solemn oath. If Ralph Monthermer's body is brought back on a shield, if I have to watch his corpse being lowered into the ground or be told that the snows of the north hold his mangled remains, I, Joanna, Princess of England, Countess of Gloucester, swear as God is my witness, that I shall not speak to you again. I shall publicly disown you as my father. I shall proclaim you as an assassin and a murderer for all the world to know!'

Edward stepped back. I lifted the dagger and pressed its tip under my own chin until the blood ran.

'What crime has Sir Ralph committed?' I demanded. 'Tell me. Point to any line in Scripture which claims that only this kind of man can marry this sort of woman. Where, in the writings of the great philosophers, does it say that love is constrained by birth or power?'

Edward held out his hand. 'Give me the dagger, Joanna.'

'Give me your word,' I said. 'Monthermer will not die in the north.'

The King nodded. 'You have my word. He will feel the lash of my anger but he will not die in the north.'

I threw my poignard to the floor. It clattered loudly in the silent chapel. I dabbed at the cut and licked the blood.

I don't know why I did what I did. That was the first and only time I ever felt such a rage within me. The worst cruelties of my husband had not driven me to the extremes that the King my father had, so unwilling to listen, to concede, to understand, so quick to deny to his own flesh and blood what had fired his soul and quickened his own heart. Oh, I felt so sick and weary.

The King was anxious but, even then, full of calculation. 'You cannot see Monthermer again. I have given my word, he shall not die in the north but you will never see him again!'

'Do not say that.' The tears scalded my eyes. I knelt down, hands joined. 'Father, I beg you!'

'You will be taken away.' Father sat in the sanctuary chair before the small altar as if he was in a meeting of the royal council issuing an edict. 'You will be taken away until this madness passes. Monthermer, too, will be detained. He is not what he claims to be.'

My father had trapped me into a confession

and now he would keep us apart. Slowly but surely, as water crumbles away stone, through loneliness, lies, flattery and bribery, the King hoped to get his way as he always got his way. I had spoken from the heart yet it made no difference. The King's face was set, his eyes obdurate. My temper cooled. This was a game of chess; cunning not passion must be my guide. I kept my head bowed.

'You are my daughter, Joanna.' His voice had turned weasel-soft, a sure sign of danger. 'You are a Plantagenet. You are sad, perhaps confused after the death of your husband. Time heals everything. In the meantime . . . '

I rose slowly to my feet. 'In the meantime, Father?'

'In the meantime, daughter, you will rest in a secluded place so these matters can be investigated.'

'Why investigated?' I asked. 'What is there to investigate?'

My father did not answer. He sat, one eyelid drooping, tapping his fingers on the arm of his chair.

'What matters are to be investigated, Father?' Did he know our secret? I thought of my chamber, the letters and poems I had written, the keepsakes I had hidden. The chapel door was off the latch, the key on the inside. I walked slowly towards my father.

'I asked you a question, Sire. What is there to investigate?'

And then, before he could react, I picked up the hem of my gown and ran towards the door.

'Joanna!' My father turned in the chair.

I already had the key out. I slammed the door shut and turned the key. I could hear my father shouting, his fists pounded the door. I threw the key down the steps and fled. My father had been so confident. At the bottom a group of royal archers were waiting but they were too startled to stop me. I pushed through them, for who, without the King's permission, would dare touch a Princess of England? I hastened across the mud-spattered courtyard and up the stairs of the keep. I passed Ricaud and Tibault. From their sly glances, I realised how busy their tongues had been. At last I reached my own chamber. I locked and barred the door, threw a log upon the fire then rifled my caskets and coffers and burnt everything I could. I heard a gentle rapping on the door.

'Go away!' I screamed.

'My lady, please, it is Alicia.'

I opened the door and let her in.

'A servant told me you were seen running across the courtyard.' She stared round at the overturned coffers and caskets. 'My lady?'

'Hush!' I pressed a finger against her lips. 'You must not stay here, Alicia. The King knows.'

Now she became frightened. The blood drained from her face, she swayed slightly, clutching her stomach. 'They will take me. They will put me to the question.'

'They will do nothing of the sort!' I snapped. I grasped her chilled hand and looked into her frightened brown eyes. 'You know nothing,' I whispered. 'You know nothing at all.'

'But — '

'Believe it, Alicia. Tell yourself you know nothing. If you know nothing you can say nothing, about Earl Gilbert's death, or Sir Ralph, or me or anyone.'

'The children?' she gasped.

'They will stay with the King at Westminster. They will be safe. The King is in a rage but he will not touch my children. Now think, Alicia,' I urged. 'Do you have anything, even the smallest scrap of evidence, that might prove you are lying?'

She closed her eyes and shook her head. I heard the distant clink of armour from the courtyard below. Alicia looked past me to the fire where the hungry yellow flames consumed the parchments.

'My lady, what are you doing?'

'Burning everything I have. I must protect Sir Ralph.'

'Is he taken?'

'He will be.' I pushed her towards the door. 'Now if you love me, Alicia, say nothing about the priest, about what you know.'

I unlocked the door and let her out. Oh, my beloved, I did what I could! I burnt the letters, the keepsakes, but I could not find the fillet for my hair that you gave me or the match to the glove I gave you. I ignored the wrench in my heart as the fire destroyed the symbols of our love. I heard a knock on the door but ignored it. Then a pounding, like that of a mailed fist.

'My lady!' I recognised Ricaud's voice. 'I'm here with your father's guards. I beg you, let me enter!'

I gazed round the room then remembered the ring. I took it from beneath the bolster and hurriedly threw it towards the fire — there was no time to hide it. I unlocked the door and opened it. The gallery outside was full of men-at-arms, swords drawn, some carrying pitch torches. Ricaud stood next to the captain, his pale, furrowed face a mask of concern but a malicious glee enlivened those dead, black eyes.

'Master Ricaud, you may come in. The

others will have to wait.'

The captain of the guard was about to protest but Ricaud raised a hand and slipped softly into my chamber. He gazed around, his eyes hungry for information. He had never been here before. I had always kept him at a distance; I had disliked him from the first and time had not improved my regard for him. Ricaud was a veritable snake in the grass, a whisperer in corners, a peerer through fingers, a man with an unhealthy appetite for malicious gossip. How does such a man justify himself? How does he sleep at night? How does he reconcile his soul to the Lord Christ? Sometimes I would attend his Mass. I always felt distant as if observing the ritual rather than a sacrament. But you know my thoughts of him. I would no more ask him to shrive me than his good friend and confidant Tibault the seneschal. Father Benedict the village priest has the care of my soul and the key to it is held by you.

Ricaud brushed past me, rejoicing in his new-found power and my disgrace.

'My lady, your father is angry.'

'You speak of my Lord the King?' I retorted. 'Father Ricaud, this is not your chapel but my chamber. You will stand still and not move without my permission. I have not met you today, Father Ricaud.'

I extended my hand for him to kiss. As he moved to do so, I lowered my hand so he had to stoop. 'I am Joanna, Princess of England, Countess of Gloucester. What do you want with me, priest?'

His look was malevolent, reminding me of a carrion crow on a gibbet post.

'You never liked me, did you?' he said.

'Like? *Like?*' This man was beneath contempt. He, among others, had poisoned my father's mind against me. 'Father Ricaud, I hardly ever notice you.'

Harsh words but I had no time for this second Judas, this spy behind the arras. I did not wish to fence and parry with him.

'If you are here to give me spiritual comfort.' I went and sat in my chair, sitting erect as if I was preparing to be crowned rather than be imprisoned. 'Then you are wasting your time. I have nothing to say to you, priest, and unless you are a messenger, I demand that you leave my chamber.' I raised a finger. 'You are not here to preach, are you? To sermonise? To give me good advice? You are a page boy, aren't you?' I continued remorselessly, 'you bring messages from my father.'

He opened his mouth to reply.

'Be careful, priest.'

'You are to be taken to the convent of

St Mary's, Malmesbury, and be placed in the custody of its Abbess, Lady Emma. You may take a few essential possessions and must leave within the hour.'

'And will I take my maid?' I regretted the question as soon as I uttered it.

His face took on a spiteful cast. 'No maid and only one set of saddlebags.'

'My children?'

Again the spiteful twist to the mouth. Ricaud pushed one leg forward and bowed. 'As you say, my lady, I am only a messenger and that is all I can say.'

'Then get out! Until I leave this castle, Father Ricaud, I am its lady. I do not want to see you or Master Tibault again. Tell the captain of the guard I shall be with him shortly.' I gestured towards the door. 'Be gone and close that behind you.'

He slammed it shut. I heard raised voices along the gallery. I tidied my chamber and filled two saddlebags. I took what I could. I wrapped a lock of your hair, the piece I cut last Twelfth Night, in vellum and hid it in the toe of one of my slippers. I looked for the ring but could not find it and wondered if it had fallen into the fire grate. I could not do anything about it. I changed for travelling. I looked round my chamber once more, breathed a prayer to you and walked out into the gallery. Mailed men gathered round me, their faces hidden beneath their helmets. The air reeked of sweat, leather and horse.

'Does my father wish to see me?'

'We are to leave now, my lady.' The captain of the guard looked fierce in his helmet but his eyes were soft. 'Our horses are ready.'

It was a cold, harsh night ride, though the soldiers of my escort were courteous enough. We made just one stop and arrived at St Mary's at Malmesbury late in the afternoon. I was delivered into the hands of 'Lady Cold Eyes', my private name for our worthy Abbess.

Early on the morning before your letter came, I began this one and wrote about what had happened on that dreadful Candlemas Eve. Then I lay back on the bed, my mind still full of what had happened, and I fell into a half-sleep. A knock roused me and I opened the door to find Sister Veronica and Sister Agnes standing together in the passageway like twin gargoyles, their wizened faces framed by starched white wimples. Each was dressed in a blue gown with a white girdle round the waist, their rosary beads wrapped about gnarled fingers.

They looked at me in surprise and I

realised I was still dressed in my nightshift, my cropped hair tousled. I plucked at it and remembered how long and golden it used to be.

'My lady,' said Sister Veronica, recovering her composure, 'you were missed at devotions and morning mass.'

Sister Agnes waggled a bony finger at me. 'The Lady Abbess wishes to see you about something important. Can we come in?'

'Yes, can we come in?' Sister Veronica echoed.

And, before I could reply, they were inside my chamber. They settled themselves on a bench beside the door and quietly watched me as I washed myself, combed my hair and took from the lavender chest a clean shift, robes and wimple.

'You must carry your beads.' Sister Agnes shook hers. 'The Lady Abbess likes to see us with our beads.'

'How long have you been here?' I asked curiously.

'Fifteen years,' said Sister Agnes.

'Eighteen,' Veronica supplied triumphantly.

'And are you happy?' I asked from behind the small screen, struggling to pull the shift over my head. I looked round. They were staring at each other.

'Happy?' Veronica's eyes rounded. 'We

96

women, my lady, are not born to be happy.'

'You must not call me my lady but Sister Joanna, otherwise Lady Cold Eyes — ' My fingers flew to my mouth. 'I am sorry,' I apologised.

'Oh, don't worry.' Sister Agnes smiled in a display of fine red gums. 'Sister Veronica calls the Lady Emma Vinegar Face. I prefer Lady of the Prunes. But she's not so bad. I've heard stories, you know . . . ' She paused at the sound of a bell chiming and the murmur of voices from the cloister garth below.

'What stories?' I asked.

'Like us, she was crossed in love.' Sister Agnes shook her head. 'Such bitterness never comes from life.'

I stepped from behind the wooden screen.

'You are here for love, aren't you?' Sister Agnes went on. 'You are not alone, you know. Look around. I mean, there is Sister — '

'Hush now!' Sister Veronica grasped her companion's thin wrist. 'We are not supposed to talk of such things. And why should we? We are past love now. I mean, what man would look at us and feel a stirring in the loins? But you are still beautiful, my lady — Sister Joanna. I can see your body is full and ripe.' She sighed. 'Mine was once. A young squire, handsome as the sun, once said that if I allowed him to kiss my fingers

97

he would take poison.'

'You never told me this!' Sister Agnes exclaimed.

'His name was Piers. He was a Breton. I allowed him to kiss my hand, gave him a tainted drink, then locked him in a cupboard.'

'And was it poison?' I asked.

'No. Just a herbal potion to purge the bowels.' Sister Veronica laughed behind her fingers. 'He was in that cupboard for hours. He never bothered me again.'

I finished my dressing, drew up a stool and sat down and studied these two old ladies. Their faces were lined with age but their eyes were bright, full of life.

'Did you love?' I asked curiously.

'Oh yes!' Both of them chorused.

'You are English?' I asked.

'No.' Sister Agnes shook her head. 'We have lost all trace of accent. We didn't meet, Veronica and I, till we came here and yet we were born only a short distance from each other, in two small villages outside Bordeaux. Isn't life a wheel? It goes round and takes you back to your first beginnings.

They clasped each other's hands. They reminded me of two young scullery maids whispering about their swains, rather than two venerable nuns who, according to their vows, had pledged their lives to Christ. I wondered what had brought them to this place after a life that included four husbands for Sister Agnes and six for Sister Veronica.

'Have you ever heard of Maraichnage?' Sister Agnes asked me.

I shook my head.

'It's a Gascon custom. On a fixed evening of every week, usually Saturday, all the eligible maids of our village were allowed to open their bedchamber door or window to the local gallants.' She saw the disbelief in my eyes. 'Oh, yes it's true. Naturally, during the week, you've chosen your man.' She shrugged one shoulder. 'You know the way it is: a look, a half-glance, a slight touch, a blown kiss. Anyway, the favoured one was allowed to come and lie on the bed beside you.' She smiled. 'Always fully clothed. We'd spend the night talking, flirting, sleeping in each other's arms.' She paused. 'Intercourse was expressly forbidden. Sometimes a rope was tied above the knees, or little bells attached to the legs of the bed. One beautiful May Sunday evening a group of young knights came to our village and camped in the fields outside. During the week I paraded through the village, swaying my hips and playing the saucebox. Then I met him — the man I gave my heart to.

'One of your husbands?' I asked.

'Oh no,' she said dismissively and continued with her story. 'I can remember everything about him, even though it's over fifty years ago. He had russet hair, a sharp face but laughing blue eyes, very bright eyes, full of life, and a smiling mouth. He was clean-shaven, his hair shorn above his ears. 'Hey, pretty one!' he called out. I stopped and talked, and when I walked away I was deeply in love. He came to my bedroom. He was dressed in a jerkin of green murrey, the shirt beneath finely embroidered, red woollen hose and leather riding boots. His spurs clinked as he climbed the ladder to my bedchamber. We lay that night side by side locked in each other's arms. My mother came in and tied a girdle round my ankles. I recall her smiling sadly at me. She knew I was in love. My beloved and I kissed but it was chastely. We hugged and embraced and, when dawn came, he left. The following afternoon he and his companions rode out of the village.

'In autumn, just before the feast of Michaelmas, I learned from a chapman who came wandering through the village that my beloved and the other knights had been ambushed by the Basques in one of the mountain passes. They were all dead. I don't even know his name, I never asked, but every night, before I fall asleep, he comes to me, and every time I made love to my husbands, in truth I was making love to him.' Sister Agnes looked at me. 'When you love like that, my lady, you must never let go.'

'Tell her your secret.' Sister Veronica nudged her.

'No, not yet.' Sister Agnes smiled at me. 'Maybe when I know you better.'

The bell began to toll again and my two visitors suddenly became agitated.

'Come on, we must go,' said Sister Veronica urgently. 'We must not be late for the chapter meetings.'

'I thought the Lady Abbess wanted to see me,' I said.

'Yes, but after the meeting. A punishment is to be carried out.'

I followed Sister Veronica and Sister Agnes out into the corridor and down the steps. I had heard of these punishments but had never witnessed one. We went out through the cloisters. I glanced at my rose, now in full bloom in its bush in the centre of the garden. I had assumed we were going to the chapter house but we skirted that and entered a dusty, paved yard near the stables. On one side stood the Lady Abbess with her nuns, and to their right and left a line of novices and lay sisters. We hurriedly took our places.

Lady Emma pulled a small silver bell from the voluminous sleeve of her gown and rang it. The door to one of the outhouses opened. A lay sister, dressed simply in a white shift and carrying a huge rock, staggered out. Behind her came another sister with a sharp stick. Each time the poor girl in front stumbled or dropped the boulder, she received a vicious prod. I looked away until the punishment was finished.

'Let it be noted,' Lady Emma proclaimed, 'that coarse and spiteful language is not acceptable in this house of God and place of prayer!'

'Nor is a pointed stick,' Sister Agnes whispered, 'or punishments like that.'

We left the yard and processed solemnly into the chapter house. Lady Emma sat in a throne-like chair, her officers clustered about. The rest of the nuns and I filed into the stalls on either side. A prayer was said and then we sang a hymn, vilely as usual. Why do high-born ladies believe that all singing must be through the nose?

The normal business of the convent was dealt with and then the Lady Abbess asked for all who had committed any misdemeanours to come forward, prostrate themselves and confess their sins. A line of penitents came forward. They all seemed to have committed the same 'sin' — eating too much in the refectory or not sharing gifts, brought by outsiders, with the other sisters.

'Is there anyone else?' the Lady Abbess called and looked at me.

I glared back. What did she expect me to do? Come and prostrate myself, tell her what had broken my heart and shattered my life?

'Ignore her,' Sister Veronica, seated behind, whispered. 'Remember, my lady, you may be wearing the habit but you have not taken the vows of a nun.'

I did not need to be reminded. I held the Lady Abbess's cold stare until she looked away. She clapped her hands and declared the business of the chapter concluded.

'Sister Joanna.' This time she did not even look in my direction. 'I require words with you in my chamber.' She then processed out of the chapter house, holding her head as if she wore an imperial crown.

I took my time and the Lady Abbess made little attempt to hide her impatience when I knocked on the door. She snapped at me to come in.

She sat behind a great oak desk littered with manuscripts, quills, inkpots and a coloured psalter on a book rest to one side. She was dictating a letter to one of the tenants of the far flung estates of the convent. She bade me sit, and then I had to wait until she had finished.

'I'll seal the letter later, Sister,' she told the nervous-looking almoner who glanced fearfully at me, picked up her writing tray and fled from the room.

Lady Emma looked through the parchments on her desk. She plucked out your letter and propped it against the book rest. The vellum was stained but I recognised your hand.

'This,' she tapped the letter with her finger as if it was a piece of dirt, 'was brought late last night by a merchant. I have not opened it.'

'Are you under instruction to read my letters, Domina?' I asked, using her formal Latin title. 'Has my father the King instructed you to open what I receive and supervise what I write?'

That cold, alabaster face remained impassive. The Lady Abbess is in fact quite beautiful. Her sea-grey eyes under plucked brows are compelling and her face is perfect, unmarked by wrinkle or blemish — and apparently incapable of breaking into a smile.

'May I have my letter?' I stretched out my hand.

'In a moment. I have also received notification from the court that your father is sending a Franciscan, Roger of Evesham, to have words with you.'

'Then I'll have words with him, Domina. Please, may I have my letter?'

'In a little while,' she replied. 'I also wish to ask.' She forced a smile. 'If you are happy here?'

'Of course I'm not!'

She seemed pleased by that.

'I know something, Sister Joanna, of the reasons for your stay here.'

'Then, Domina, you may understand my pain.'

'Pain?' She arched an eyebrow. 'What is so painful about being Countess of Gloucester and daughter of the King?'

I did not deign to answer. My gaze wandered to the small table at the other side of the desk and the polished, gleaming skull resting there on a blue velvet cloth edged with gold. The Lady Abbess followed my gaze.

'A memento mori,' she said, picking up the skull. She turned it slowly. 'It is said that this belonged to a young novice, Philippa atte Churche. Her parents put her here because she became infatuated with a local knight. According to legend — '

'I have heard the story,' I interrupted. 'She went into the maze that forms part of the convent gardens and committed suicide. The nuns here, with their usual charity, would not bury her corpse in consecrated ground and allowed her skull to become a plaything for future abbesses.'

She flinched at the contempt in my voice.

'And I've heard the rumours,' I continued. 'The ghost of poor Philippa still haunts that maze.' I couldn't check my temper. 'Don't you have any compassion?' I almost shouted. 'Are you hinting that the same fate is reserved for me? Do you know,' and I was glad to see a gleam of fear, 'that I am a Princess of England? How dare you bring me in here to threaten and bait me? You are consecrated to Christ. Good God, I've met tricksters with more compassion in their little fingernail than you have in your entire body.'

'I am Abbess here.'

'Yes and God help everybody else!' I shouted. 'Was there any real need for that cruelty this morning? A young woman carrying a boulder, being prodded by a sharpened stick in the buttocks? In God's name, if that's what happens in our nunneries, how dare you object to what my father does to rebels in Wales!'

'Your father said that you were subject to my authority.'

'Do you really understand why I am here, Domina?'

She nodded imperceptibly.

'I loved a man. I fell deeply and hopelessly in love with a man better, finer, stronger and braver than any other man I have met. My love is vibrant, it is pure. Haven't you ever loved?'

'I love the Lord Jesus,' she said, her face taut.

'So did Mary Magdalene. She kissed his feet. She embraced him. She anointed his body. Could you do that? Or can you only worship pieces of wood and stone?'

Her lower lip quivered, like a child about to burst into tears.

My eyes strayed to the precious piece of parchment still lying on the desk. I could have reached across and plucked it up but I wanted her to give it to me.

'Have you ever loved?' I pressed on. 'Man or woman? Old or young?'

She looked up at the ceiling, swallowing rapidly, as if she was fighting back a sob.

'Once,' she whispered. 'Just once.' She brought her head down. 'I loved and I lost.' She clasped the silver crucifix which hung on a gold chain round her neck. 'So, before you judge and condemn me, Joanna, Princess of England, I really do know something of your pain. I come from good family, the Howards of Norfolk. I was raised with many brothers and sisters but my parents, though noble, were poor, and could not afford a dowry for me.' She glanced away. 'So, what shall we do with poor Emma? they asked. Who will have her without a dowry? I was narrow-waisted and flat-breasted, a poor prospect in the marriage market. Then I went and did something stupid. I fell in love. His name was Philip Escures, a poor knight. He owned a manor whose roof had more holes than tiles and land that was harsh and infertile. He was ten years my senior but he had a kindly face, a ready wit and he was a nimble dancer.' She brought her hands to her lips as if in prayer. 'I would have married him but he was considered unsuitable for a Howard. Poor Emma thinks she can live like a peasant, what shall we do with her? I was forbidden any contact with Escures and my father arranged for me to be admitted to a convent outside Norwich. I proved to be an exemplary novice, and for the first time in my life I was free of that terrible refrain, 'What shall we do with poor Emma?' ' She tapped the desk with her fingers. 'So don't sit there in judgement on me, Joanna of England. You have known a man. You know what it is to bear children. You were given one

108

opportunity to love and now you are being offered a second.' Her lips trembled. 'I was not so fortunate.'

I sat back in the chair. I pitied her. I had mistaken the mask for the face.

'I am sorry,' I said. 'I truly am. When you are locked in pain you become blind to other people's.'

She picked up your letter and handed it to me. 'I wish you well, Joanna of England.'

I rose, bowed and walked to the door.

'Sister Joanna?'

I turned, my hand on the latch. 'We all have our tasks in this community. Since you have such strong views about the punishment you witnessed this morning, in future recalcitrant nuns and novices will be sent to you and you will decide what shall be done with them.' She nodded in dismissal. 'You may go.'

Surprised and somewhat unsettled by this turn of events, I left the Abbess's quarters clutching your letter. I was like a child with a stolen sweetmeat who wonders where to eat it. I walked quickly, smiling and nodding at those I passed. I did not want to go back to my chamber. Instead, I found myself out in the gardens and, strangely enough, heading towards the overgrown maze where Philippa atte Churche is said to have ended her life.

The day was bright and sunny, swallows skimmed the top of the privet hedges, the air was sweet with the fragrance of flowers and herbs.

Deep inside the maze I eventually stopped and sat on the ground. The sharp privet pricked the back of my head. I examined the seal. It seemed untouched. I slipped my finger under the wax and watched it crack. I slowly unfolded the parchment.

I don't know how long I stayed there, reading and re-reading your letter. I was aware of the shadows growing longer, the breeze turning cold, the distant bells calling the nuns to church or to the refectory. I got slowly to my feet and found my muscles ached. A shadow caught my eye as if someone was flitting through the maze, playing a childish game of hide and seek with me. I thought of poor Philippa atte Churche. This was no place to read your letter, to understand and savour every word. I brushed the grass and dirt from my gown and headed back the way I had come — or so I thought. For in a little while, I was lost. A strange fancy entered my mind: that I would go round and round and they would never find me. Clutching your letter in my hand, I laughed at myself — that is what comes of listening to too many romantic stories.

'I am Joanna of England!' I shouted to the sky. 'I will survive! One day I shall meet Ralph again!' A bird skimming over the maze seemed to answer my shout.

In a short while, I was free of that dark place. The convent was silent, I had missed the midday meal but I knew where I should go.

I entered the chapel. It was empty, the incense swirling around like forgotten prayers. I went up the transept, took a taper and lit a candle before the statue of the Virgin. I have never before seen a statue like this one. The Virgin Mother is depicted as a young woman no more than sixteen or seventeen summers; she sits cradling a child like I would cradle mine.

I put the candle on the brass holder, stood back and stared. I meant to give thanks for your letter but, instead, I recalled my own children. I missed them. I truly did. I wanted them with me. I wanted to sit them down in front of me, embrace them and tell them what had happened, affirm that I loved them. The Lady Emma would no doubt find that difficult to believe. Never once had I begged to see my own children. We truly are, as the preacher says, a mixture of light and dark.

I love all three of my children, Ralph, you know that. But the manner of their conception is like a barrier between us. Standing alone before that wooden statue, my candle burning fiercely, I thought of my husband, Gilbert de Clare, and I suddenly felt truly free of him. He was dead. He would never come back. As you know, ever at Tonbridge I would sometimes jump with fear. Was that his footstep outside? Would he come swaggering into the hall, thumbs in his sword belt, cloak thrown over his shoulder to stare at me with those crazed eyes? And when I woke with a start in the middle of the night, was it the cry of some night bird that had disturbed me or de Clare fighting the demons which prowled his soul?

I knelt down and said a prayer. Then I left the chapel. The cloister was deserted; the nuns of St Mary's were taking their afternoon rest. I went and crouched beside my rose. I held it to my cheek, as I would my lips to your ear, with my hand resting on your heart. I wanted to tell it all the passion I felt for you. I knelt there like a good nun in prayer and re-read your letter greedily, taking each word like a thirsty man would precious water yet, like him, craving more.

I smiled and quietly cheered at your brave, mad escape though I wept at your taking. Did you really think you could charge south and free me like some errant knight? Swoop down like the hawk you are? Would you have arrived, sweat-soaked and mud-covered, to thunder at the gates of the nunnery as you did the door of my heart? Snatch me up, pierce me through with a sweetness that is past all understanding? Oh, your courage strengthens me. And yet you must be careful. You must be prudent and treasure your life as I do. Remember, I live in you and you in me. My heart only beats in echo to yours. We are no longer two but one, flesh and blood separate yet joined through the web of life.

My father is well-named the leopard of England. Once, shortly before my marriage to de Clare, the King took me to the Tower where some powerful Prince of Tartary had sent him a beautiful leopard as a gift. The grounds of the Tower had been cleared, the leopard released and some poor animal, a deer caught in the nearby forest, brought in to serve as prey. My father made me watch the hunt. Oh, the courage of the leopard, its speed, but all I truly remember is its cunning. My father the King is like that: a creature of the night as well as Prince of the light.

I miss you so much. I also miss Alicia and those other friends, the people who made up our lives at Tonbridge.

As I've said, I miss my babies but, in truth, they seem distant. I wondered about that in the convent chapel and do so again. Am I not their mother? Are they not flesh of my flesh? Have I not given birth and suckled them at my breast? Has my heart turned to stone? I weep at the very thought of them.

I cannot act the hypocrite. Gilbert the Red is dead, his shadow-filled life is ended. Both that, and his death, divide me from what is mine. The great de Clare lies cold beneath the freezing effigy of Tonbridge and, for all I care, his soul can sit on some fiery rock in Purgatory and seethe at me as he did in life. An old woman once told me that, at twilight, ghosts are allowed to wander back, to sit and watch the living. Does de Clare's soul come looking for vengeance? Does he blame me for his death? Perhaps he is right to do so but God will absolve me, for God understands all. Every man whistles up his own end and de Clare did his. He built his own chamber of Hell and thronged it with his grievances and hatred. His two disciples, Ricaud and Tibault, remain; I fear they will do me no good.

I have read your letter again. One name prickles the skin on the nape of my neck, Henry Trokelowe. Beware of Trokelowe. I have not met him but I have heard much about him. Trokelowe is a trusted clerk of the Royal Chapel, the custodian of the

114

King's secrets, guide and adviser to the royal conscience. The King often mentioned him and so did de Clare. When my husband talked of affairs of state and said how the King had decided this or that, he would usually add, 'But of course, he will ask Trokelowe's advice.'

One incident I do recall. My husband was despatched by the King to investigate a great robbery at St Olave's shrine in Essex. He was accompanied by specially appointed commissioners. Now St Olave's held a special reliquary which hung on a silver chain in a small side chapel at the back of the priory just within the west door. It was watched by two of the brothers who knelt at the altar rails. Pilgrims would throng to the shrine to pay their respects. One evening the reliquary disappeared, and no one could understand how it had happened.

Earl Gilbert and his advisers could make no sense of it either. The reliquary had disappeared while the church was empty of pilgrims. The two good brothers on prayerful vigil before it could not be suspected for they were the ones who raised the alarm. Earl Gilbert informed the King who despatched Trokelowe to St Olave's. He made careful investigation. For days he questioned the brothers and inspected documents. My husband said it was like a beehive being turned over. In the end Trokelowe trapped the librarian, the monk in charge of the scriptorium. He found certain drawings hidden away and asked Father Prior's permission for the two monks, who had been custodians of the shrine, to take their place at the altar rail. He also made careful examination of the beautiful rose windows which lay behind the shrine. The Prior had no choice but to agree and Trokelowe waited.

Trokelowe declared the first and second evenings were not suitable. On the third, he announced to the surprised Prior that he wanted no one in the church except the two brothers who'd been there when the reliquary had been stolen. He also explained how he would hang a piece of parchment on the hook which held the reliquary and that no one would see it. The Prior laughed but Trokelowe was insistent.

The two brothers began their watch. The others were told to go about their normal business, even my husband and the judges were excluded. The two watchers knelt on their prie-dieus. An hour passed and, shortly before the bell rung for compline, just as the sun set, the two guardians were surprised to see a piece of parchment dangling from the hook. Their consternation roused the rest of the community.

Trokelowe summoned them all into the shrine. He showed them that on each side of the shrine, a small transept sealed by a door which could be opened. The Prior replied that these doors were not locked because the reliquary was watched both day and night, so how could any thief enter without the alarm being raised? Trokelowe's solution was simple. He pointed out how the chapel faced west, being opposite the high altar. The rose window behind the reliquary was full of brilliantly coloured glass and, when the sun set, the shrine was dazzled with light. The good Prior was highly doubtful but Trokelowe appealed to those brothers who had taken the watch at that particular hour. They all confessed, without exception, that the rose-red window was so dazzling, in a fiery sunset it hurt their eyes and they were forced to look away. Trokelowe intervened to placate the Father Prior's anger and asked if any wise man would dare look at the sun direct. Father Prior admitted that no one would but remained unconvinced.

Trokelowe had to wait two further evenings for another glorious sunset. This time he and Father Prior, together with my husband, knelt before the altar rail. At sunset, even though my husband did not wish to do so, the dazzling light forced him to look away for a period which would take the space of ten Aves to fill. It was almost impossible to see the altar or the reliquary chain above it.

The thief had also noticed this: the angle of the sun, the brilliance of the light and its effect upon the watchers. He must have come through the side door and removed the reliquary. Both Father Prior and my husband were convinced. Trokelowe concluded it must be a member of the community, someone who had closely studied this phenomena. He produced the writings he had found in the scriptorium and the librarian was closely questioned. The man confessed that he was a collector of curios and artefacts and always wished to possess the reliquary for himself. He had studied the angle of the setting sun and the effulgence it caused which seemed to draw a veil across the altar and the reliquary above it. The librarian also admitted how, dressed in white and wearing soft-soled sandals, it was easy to cross the floor at such a time, go up behind the altar and, in a few seconds, detach the reliquary from its chain.

I remember it well. My husband seldom laughed but, for days after his return, he marvelled at Trokelowe's subtlety.

If the King has commissioned this clerk

to probe our love and question you, then be careful! This is not a man who uses a branding iron or red-hot pincers; his tools are a very sharp wit and infinite patience. He will sit and quietly question, leading you down paths and byways you would not wish to go. If Trokelowe is now involved, the King intends to lay quiet siege to our love. Trokelowe will stretch out hidden nets to catch your thoughts like a hunter does conies in the hay.

As for me, I await the arrival of the Franciscan, Roger of Evesham. Perhaps my father thinks my love will falter under the pious guidance of this friar. Foolish hope. My love grows stronger every day; no monkish entreaty will touch it.

Do not grieve for me, Ralph. The life of the convent is a distraction and the good sisters, though vowed to Christ, still, despite all their protests, live in the world of men. As I have written before, there is lively humour here and in the refectory the wine is good and we are well fed, though the interminable tracts we are made to listen to do little for the digestion. The convent receives many visitors, particularly scholars travelling to and from France. One of these brought the Lady Abbess *Les Lamentations de Mahieu*. The book was intended to instruct the good sisters on the purity of their lives as set against the travails of marriage. The writer, and you may reflect on this, demanded that every marriage should have a trial period of a year; a man should be able to try out his wife before committing himself to a lifelong habit. Marriages, in essence, should have novices, as in any monastery or convent, and final vows should be taken only after a period of careful reflection. Would to God that was so! The writer seemed to believe that God was a bachelor and argued that in Heaven married men be ranked higher than the angels because of the martyrdom they had been through! In hushed but merry discussion afterwards the good sisters thought otherwise.

'Martyrdom?' Sister Veronica exclaimed. 'I'll give the nincompoop martyrdom! What does he know about beery breath and ham-like fists?'

'Hush now,' Sister Agnes warned. 'If Lady Prune Face hears of our frivolity on the subject we'll have to listen to the lamentations of Job and there's very little humour in that.'

I do not doubt that the Lady Abbess has spies among the community. Certainly *The Lamentations of Mahieu* were swiftly replaced with monkish reflections on Hell and Purgatory. Who could the spy be? Sister Catherine who was a merchant's wife in Bristol? Sister Anne who constantly boasts how her late departed husband was Sheriff of Gloucester? Sister Agnes or Sister Veronica even? I often wonder why any of them came here. Why do such women give up comfortable widowhood to live in a place like this?

I ventured to ask Sister Agnes. She tells me it is because they are weary of living in the world of men. 'We were used like counters on the marriage table and had no choice or control over our lives.'

'But these sisters are wealthy women from high-ranking families.'

'Indeed,' smiled Sister Agnes. 'Like you, Lady Joanna. And when your husband died, were you free to do what you wanted, go where you wanted, love whom you wanted?'

I could only smile in reply. She had hit the mark fair and square.

Sister Agnes grasped my hand between her cold, gnarled fingers. 'I was married more times than I care to think. Not once was it for love. No sooner was the funeral ceremony over than powerful kinsmen would throng to the door, introducing this person or that. And when your body becomes dry and cracked and you think you are free, there are the children, except they are now full grown. I have children.' She looked away. 'Sons may mean well but they wish you to go here or go there. 'You can have that chamber, you can eat with us in the hall today.' ' She shook her head. 'At least here we have some freedom, some calm, some rest from the constant importuning.'

'Are you sad?' I asked. 'Is your life full of regrets?'

'I regret one thing only.' Sister Agnes drew closer. 'That I never grasped what love offered me.' She ran her finger along my cheek. 'Remember that, Joanna of England.'

I shall and I do. I am resolved in my love for you. I will love you or I will die. So love me for love's eternity and if you fall, my falcon dove, then I shall fall with you, down past the woven, gold-shot fabric of this world. So, even death does not frighten me, if death brings me to you. Remember this.

Written at Malmesbury, the feast of Pachomius, 1297.

Letter 5

From Henry Trokelowe to Edward the King, health and greetings.

This matter now moves on apace. I will not spell it out in detail; as Your Grace knows, I am a cautious man, and if the letters of others can be deciphered and understood then why not mine? Moreover, this is a strange matter. 'A shrewd clerk' is how Your Grace described me, as well as one knowledgeable in lovesickness. Yet is this a matter of lovesickness? Of genuine love between a man and a woman irrespective of their status? Or is it really a question of the law, of adultery and murder? At this moment I am certain that love is the cause and origin of all that had happened.

When I go fishing, I cast my line and hook, and I wait. Sometimes you go fishing for one species and find another, or sit for an hour and hook more in that time than you did the previous day. That's what I like about fishing, it's a mixture of luck and logic and these two will be the key here. Luck, in that I may discover something, logic that I may build a pattern, a train of thought which will lead me to the truth. I need these two because love is a difficult fish to hook and, even when you catch it, slippery to grasp.

Fishermen and lovers have a great deal in common. Both tell stories of what could or might have been. I remember a fellow clerk in the Chancery. He was travelling with messages to the Sheriff of York and stopped at a tavern where he met the fairest of damsels. At supper time he sat by himself while she and her companions feasted on the other side of the taproom. During the evening she cast him long and languorous glances. He did not know what to do and did not take the matter up. When he returned to Westminster, he talked about it for days, describing the fair lady in every detail. He marvelled at the turn of her mouth, the cast of her eyes, how delicate her fingers, how narrow her waist; he was truly ravished by the thought of what might have, could have, should have happened. I laughed at his tale. He grew angry and asked me why I was amused. I replied that he reminded me of a fisherman who had netted the fattest carp only to see it slip away.

I wondered then, and still do now, what love is. What is this deadly, heart-stopping contagion which smites high and low? It can turn the mind and blind the eye, put a man's soul up for sale and shatter the habits of a lifetime. Is it an invisible sprite or demon of the air? Why does it smite one and yet spare another?

I was born, as Your Grace knows, the only son of a London merchant who dealt in leather and fabric. My mother died before I could remember her but my father was a kindly man and, in his own way, tried to fill the emptiness. I was studious, and he was delighted that I spent more time among the parchment-makers and book-sellers around St Paul's than playing boyish games. I had a hunger for books like other youths do for wine, food or the joys of the bed. The learning of the ancients, the writings of Augustine, Aquinas, even those Moorish philosophers Averroes and Avicenna, did not escape my hungry interest.

'Henry, are you to be a priest?' my father's business acquaintances would ask as I sat in some corner, the candles lit around me, leafing through some manuscript or book.

'You'd make a good priest,' one of them declared.

'Why?' I asked. 'Because I like books?'

My father looked at me strangely. I remember the occasion well. The rain was pattering on the casement window and I had run from school to show him what I had bought.

'What is it you want to be, Henry?' my father asked. 'I thought you would be a priest.'

The answer came before I could stop it. 'To be a priest, Father, one must love God. But how can I love God whom I have not seen when I find it difficult to love my fellow man whom I do see?'

My father's friends clapped and praised my wit but, on that evening, with the rain pelting down, for the first time ever I had shown my father the emptiness in my heart.

The months passed. My school, which met in one of the side chapels of St Paul's, could do no more for me. The canon in charge, a scholarly man, advised my father that I be sent to study the Quadrivium, the logic and philosophy of Aristotle, in the Halls of Oxford. I needed no second bidding. In my sixteenth summer I left my father's house and joined the other scholars in Redfern Hall which stands behind Carfax. I wore the bachelor's robe, hired a chamber and attended the disputations in the schools.

I was lonely, I found it difficult to make friends. I could not hold my ale and had no inclination to fight with dagger and club along the mud-packed runnels of Oxford.

One day a new scholar came to our house, Crispin Fitz-Warren, tall and red-haired, with piercing blue eyes and a nose broken in some youthful escapade. Like me, he was a merchant's son but he possessed all the social graces I lacked. He was witty, skilled in sharp repartee, of excellent memory and conversant in Latin, French and even a little Greek. He became the leader of the scholars, a generous man ever ready to help others, always prepared to support the weak. The wenches adored him, the other scholars regarded him as they would a prince or king. Sometimes, when we ate in the common hall, I would catch him studying me closely, not in a hostile or offensive manner, but sadly, as if he could read my thoughts and recognised my loneliness.

One day the Masters of our Hall, I think it was the feast of Corpus Christi, invited us to a great banquet in the principal refectory. The tables were arranged around the dais, covered in white cloths, bearing the arms and insignia of the college. Pewter cups and platters, ivory-handled knives, chased silver jugs of wine had been laid out and the air was full of savoury smells from the buttery and kitchen. Crispin, I and others from our house took our seats. Now, as usual, I was shy and embarrassed. In my haste I picked up the finger bowl, believing it was a cup of water and, before I realised my mistake, sipped from it. This provoked merriment among the rest and I blushed at my ignorance. Crispin, sitting opposite, immediately picked up his own finger bowl.

'What I dip into,' he announced, 'I always drink from first.' He swallowed the water in one gulp.

Of course, the others followed suit. Crispin smiled and winked across the table. I suppose for lesser kindnesses many a man will enter Heaven.

The feasting began. Crispin took the opportunity to speak to me. Only on reflection did I realise how both subtle and kindly he was. He talked about the works of Roger Bacon and his theories of the stars. I, of course, like some unsuspecting fish, rose to the bait and I chattered like a child — about what I had read, what I knew, what I hoped to learn. He sat there listening, now and again nodding agreement with what I said, always ready to fill any empty silence. I was happy; for the first time in my short life, I knew what it was to belong to a group, a fraternity.

Once the feasting was over, Crispin and I walked back arm in arm to our lodgings and shared a cup of wine. It was the start of a deep friendship. Crispin and I became like brothers. (Your Grace may understand how reluctant I am to talk of this.) The friendship caused some envy and resentment, sniggers and whispers behind raised hands, but it was not like that, more like the affection between David and Jonathan whose love was beyond that of women. We studied, ate, prayed and, on occasions, wenched together. Crispin became my boon companion. I am not sure whether I was his shadow or he mine but we planned our future together. I did not wish to remain a scholar but to become a royal clerk and Crispin declared the same ambition.

Two years passed. We were like brothers until Crispin fell in love. Catherine was a beautiful young woman. Her father was a parchment-maker who supplied the university, and even the abbey at Osney, with vellum and writing materials for their scriptoria. Crispin met her on May Day, at some festival held down near the Cherwell. Never have I seen a man so lovestruck! He no longer talked about the works of the philosophers or speculated about the real nature of life or the substance of God. There was no more chatter about becoming a royal clerk. From the moment Crispin rose till the moment he fell asleep, his mind and his talk was full of Catherine. She did not spurn his advances and nor did her father. Crispin came of good family so no obstacle was placed between him and his beloved. Her father, of course, insisted that when she and Crispin met, a maid was present, and sometimes Crispin took me.

We would sit in her garden or parlour or take a stroll through Christchurch Meadows. As God is my witness, I was happy for Crispin, but I did not take to Catherine and she did not like me. Oh, she was beautiful with her heart-shaped face, unblemished skin and dark eyes full of mischief but she was born to flirtation as a fish to swimming. Catherine had a streak of cruelty in her; she was one of those people who like to see sadness in another's eyes. At first she was sweet and coy but, as Crispin's ardour became more intense, his suit more earnest, she began to play the reluctant maid and sprinkled her conversation with the names of other admirers, how this person had visited her the previous day, how an old acquaintance of her father's had brought his son to dine (her pretty eyelids would flutter) and how they had talked and gossiped about childhood days.

I tried to warn Crispin. The more I saw of Catherine, the more agitated I became. She reminded me of a cat who had caught a bird and was more intent on the play than the kill. She was the cause of our only quarrel. Sometimes, when we drank in the Blue Boar tavern or when I found Crispin alone, I would beg him to be careful, but he was smitten and as sick as any man could be with a deadly contagion.

'If I cannot have Catherine,' he declared defiantly, 'then I do not want life.'

My agitation deepened. One day I came home to find Crispin lying on his bed, sobbing like a child. Catherine had spurned his advances, stoutly declaring that she did not wish to see him again. I tried to cheer his heart and divert his mind. I gave him comfort and advice. Catherine would realise her mistake. This was surely no more than a little conceit that she would tire of.

The days passed into weeks. I even went to see her myself and for the first and only time in my life I went on my knees to beg. She heard me out, sitting round-eyed, savouring every word, rejoicing in the pain and distress she had caused. I lost my temper and called her a cold-hearted whore. She summoned the servants. I was shown the door and forbidden to return or mention my friend's name again.

'I am to be married,' she declared before the door closed. 'The betrothal day is set.'

'Who?' I asked, pushing the servants away.

'A merchant's son who holds rich estates in Norfolk.'

'When?' I asked.

She sniggered behind her hand and that was all the proof I needed. She had played with the affections of my friend, knowing full well that she was leading him up love's dark alley to the hard brick wall of her heart. I cursed her as a strumpet and one of the servants struck me before throwing me out.

When I returned to my lodgings, Crispin was waiting. I could not disguise my anger and hurt, so he had the truth from me. He became very calm, sat there nodding, as I used to when my father talked to me as a child. Crispin promised that he would forget her. He would never mention her name and would return to his studies and our student life together. I, like the fool I was, rejoiced to see his wits returned. I made him promise that the following day, after the schools were closed, he, I and others would meet in the Blue Boar where we would make the rafters ring with our songs and listen to the city bells chime at midnight.

The next day I was first in the taproom, issuing orders to the taverner and his scullions as to what tables we needed, what wines and meat were to be served. The others arrived.

They'd brought rebecs, lutes, tambours so we could sing and be merry.

The candles were lit, the boards laid out and still Crispin did not come. I was puzzled but not concerned, until one of the other students said he had seen Crispin leave the schools and hurry back to our lodgings. My heart went cold. I should have met Crispin as I left. He must have waited on the corner of the alleyway until I and the others had gone and the lodgings were empty. Fear pricked my soul. A terrible premonition chilled my blood. I leapt out of that tavern and ran as I'd never run before.

Our lodgings were empty, the front door off its latch, the small eating hall below stairs dark and gloomy. I ran up to our chamber. The door was locked and bolted. I went out into the street screaming for help. Two pedlars, in return for a penny each, came in, took a bench from the eating hall and broke down the door.

Crispin had tied a rope round one of the ceiling beams, put the noose about his neck then stepped off a stool, kicking it away. The flesh was cold, his face calm as if he'd willed himself to die as quickly as possible. I sliced the noose and rubbed his neck and chest.

'He has gone, lad,' one of the pedlars

declared. 'The soul's gone. He's been dead awhile.'

In the following weeks I learned what the mystics mean by the dark night of the soul. Time passed like a dream. Crispin's father came to Oxford and, using his influence and silver, arranged for the body to be transported to a small village outside London where it was given hallowed burial. He thanked me for what I had done and gave me a keepsake. It was the satchel, fashioned out of Cordovan leather, that Crispin had used to carry his books. He was inordinately proud of it.

I mourned him quietly, not in drunkenness or outcry, but like a mother would a child or a brother his sibling. Nightmares plagued my sleep. I used to wake in those greying hours between night and day and thought he was lying on the bed opposite, staring at me. I'd catch his face in a crowd or see it in the schools, in a tavern or cookshop.

Three months later, when the pain had begun to dull but the memory was still fresh, I heard that Catherine was to marry in St Mary's Church near Carfax. I took Crispin's satchel and filled it with dirt and soil. I waited inside the porch in the shadows by the baptismal font. Catherine entered, her bridal party all around. Pennies and flowers were thrown. Like a ghost, I stood watching her smiling, spiteful face and the fat swain she had chosen to share her bed. I chose my moment and stepped forward when she would have no choice but to see me. Her face paled and her eyes grew round, but she was more concerned that her great day might be spoilt than by any memory of Crispin.

No one stopped me as I emptied the mud and dirt at her slippered feet.

She stared at me.

'It's an old custom,' I told her.

'What do you mean?'

'When injustice is done,' I hissed, 'the earth cries out to God and demands retribution.' The men in the party were becoming restless. I ignored them. 'The grief and pain you have caused will not be forgotten and one day the earth's cry for justice will be answered.'

It was a stupid, dramatic gesture, a memory of something my father had told me, but it was the only thing I could do.

My soul became like a tree in winter which forgets how, in summer, it is clothed in leafy greenness full of sap and life. For a while I cursed all women. I regarded their smiles as spider's bites, their sweet looks as assassin's barbs. I lost myself in my studies. I won a reputation as a great scholar against whom no other would dare to dispute. Then, as

Your Grace knows, I entered your service and put my skills at your disposal.

Oh, I have changed. My temper has cooled. My resentment and hatreds are nothing but smoke from the firs of my grief. I like a pretty wench, I have women friends but no lover. A great gulf has opened between me and women, haunted by Crispin's ghost.

Crispin had everything to live for. He gambled all on love and, when he lost, gave up life itself. After his funeral I became obsessed with this. How could love turn such a man's wits? Was this an exception? Or the general effect? I could not ask others, for all you receive is an impudent answer or a witty remark. So I turned to the writings of the masters. I entered a new realm, quite different from that of philosophy or theology or mysticism. I entered the world of medicine and physic and the effect of our bodily humours on the mind. And what a world!

The Arabs talk of *ischk* which they define as an irresistible desire to obtain possession of a loved object or being. They argue that when a person falls in love and suffers from its sickness, it is because the soul sees a true reflection of itself, what it really is, and reaches out to possess it. That did not satisfy me. Too metaphysical and, when I applied it to the practicalities of life, too unlikely. Surely Crispin did not see Catherine as a reflection of himself?

The great Galen, in his work *The Prognostics*, tells of the wife of a Roman senator who, without any explanation, began to suffer from insomnia and deep agitation though no fever or morbid state could be diagnosed. Galen applied the pulse test in which he listened to the beat of the blood in the neck or wrist as he questioned her. Galen reached the conclusion that her illness was of the soul rather than the body. He observed that her pulse became disturbed and irregular whenever she mentioned the name of the dancer Polybius. Galen's story intrigued me. However, he concluded that lovesickness was only a woman's condition. I rejected this and went searching for other explanations.

I studied the writings of that great master of love Ovid who, in his poem 'The Art of Loving', talked of young lovers who, out of despair, kill themselves. They actually go mad for love. Ovid's cure was that they should slake their lust by copulation and that intercourse would bring relief. Yet Crispin's love for Catherine was more than a physical urge, a desire for the joys of the bed. And in the case of the Princess Joanna and Monthermer, we do not know if they have enjoyed intimacy.

The explanation that fascinated me most I found in Constantine the African's chapter on lovesickness in *The Viaticum*. This scholar from the Coast of Barbary wrote his great work some two hundred years ago. It has been translated and commented on by the great masters in the schools of Paris, Oxford and Cambridge, as well as the mystics who constantly argue about the difference between human love and that of God.

Constantine repeated a story from antiquity of a young man called Perdicus. As a boy, Perdicus was sent to Athens to study. He made offerings to all the gods except Venus and Cupid who were deeply offended by the way he ignored them. Years later he set out for home. After an exhausting day's journey, he and his companions turned off the road into a shady grove, to drink from a stream and take their rest. Perdicus fell asleep and the love god Cupid, outraged by Perdicus's neglect, pierced the young man's breast with a dart. An image appeared to Perdicus in his dream and he fell in love with it.

The next day, as he crossed the threshold of his house, he recognised the image in the figure who greeted him, his father's new wife, his stepmother. Perdicus was racked by incestuous desire. He could not sleep, he could not eat or drink. His limbs became weak and his worried parents called in the city physicians. Eventually they turned for help to that most famous physician, Hippocrates. He, too, was deeply puzzled by the symptoms but could discover no physical cause.

One day Hippocrates was measuring the youth's pulse when his stepmother entered the room. The pulse, which had been slow and regular, began to race. Hippocrates concluded that the cause of Perdicus's sickness was psychological, a deep, unrequited love for his stepmother.

Now this appealed to me. Perdicus fell in love with someone forbidden; he could not possibly consummate such a relationship without incurring the wrath of the gods. I remembered that never once in his courting of Catherine had he mentioned marriage. I was puzzled by this. If a young man loves a maid, he courts, he woos and eventually sets a day for betrothal and marriage. Why didn't Crispin do this? And yet, when Catherine forsook him, Crispin took his own life. Is there something about love, I wondered, which deliberately pursues the unattainable? Is that common to us all? Or just to certain people?

In a more practical fashion, does this apply to your daughter, the Lady Joanna? Has she set her heart, her mind and soul on someone whom she secretly knows she cannot attain? If that is the case further questions arise. Why has she done this? Is it because she is secretly desperate for love but frightened of it? Has the face and form of Monthermer upset the humours of her mind by provoking memories she would like to forget? My next question, Your Grace, is that if this is the case, how can it be cured? And here we are in great danger. This is my final reason for telling you, in great detail, what has happened in my life and what I have learnt.

If the Lady Joanna has set her heart on someone she cannot have, what use is there reasoning with her? Or trying to satisfy that great hunger? Could it, God forbid, also lead to madness? Perhaps even death? I am, as Your Grace knows, a clerk of the Royal Chapel, I have sworn a great oath, holding your hands in mine over the sacrament, to give you the wisest advice and counsel possible. I must therefore warn you that this is no mathematical problem with a set solution, or a mystery like that which occurred at St Olave's Priory where logic and critical observation can determine the truth. Indeed, in this matter, the more we probe the more dangerous it can become. If Joanna, by herself, or with the help and support of Monthermer, slew Earl Gilbert because of the love that existed between them, then if this love is frustrated, should they not seek death themselves? And here is the trap. If young Monthermer goes into the dark, Lady Joanna's state of mind can never be changed. If they are kept separate, their love and passion will only grow. Yet if they are brought together, you will regard that as a grave insult to both yourself and the Crown.

I write all this, Your Grace, to advise and warn you. I will of course follow your orders and pursue this matter to its logical conclusion, and establish the cause, or agent, of Earl Gilbert's death, and the exact nature and duration of the relationship between the Lady Joanna and Sir Ralph Monthermer.

At Tonbridge, after writing my last letter to you, I restlessly wandered the castle, its gardens and orchards. Darkness had fallen but I sat by the stew pond and watched fat carp nose at the surface for flies. Studying fish is soothing, it calms the black bile and restores harmony to the humours of the body and mind. Then I visited the chapel where you and the Lady Joanna had your turbulent confrontation. A cold, narrow place despite the glittering sanctuary lamps, the silver candelabra, the golden cruets and the ice-white altar cloths. I sat and prayed, though I find it difficult to clear my mind for prayer when matters here on earth can become so disjointed, corrupted and, sometimes, truly evil. However, I said my own vespers and, as I do every evening, breathed a prayer for Crispin Fitz-Warren before returning to the business in hand.

I avoided Ricaud and Tibault. They apparently want to speak to me together but that is not my way. I always choose my own time and place.

I went in search of Alicia, Lady Joanna's maid, and found her hiding in the kitchen, a dark-haired, slim-waisted girl. She was embroidering a cloth and chattering to the cooks as they built up the fires to bake tomorrow's bread. She started like a rabbit at my approach. Even in the poor light of the candle I could see her throat pulsing and the small beads of sweat beneath her head-dress. I talked to the cooks, accepted a slice of venison pie and a cup of Bordeaux which any tavern would envy. I sat opposite Alicia and, for a while, chattered about the weather. I praised her skilful stitching and wondered aloud why such a pretty girl should be sitting by herself.

'Sir,' she stammered, 'I am not by myself.'
She pointed to the sweaty-faced cooks. 'I talk
and laugh with them.'

I finished my pie and pushed the platter
away. I asked for another cup, filled it with
wine and pushed it across to her.

'Alicia, you know why I am here.'

'I have nothing to say, sir.'

She is a fragile, little thing and I praise
Your Grace's kindness towards her. Alicia
is not some bold-eyed, proud-lipped wench
prepared to give as good as she got. She is
not suited to darkened chambers and cowled
interrogators.

'Is that because you know nothing or
because you wish to tell me nothing?' I
asked.

One of the cooks drew closer to eavesdrop
but I waved him away.

'I mean you no harm.' I smiled and,
pushing back the stool, got to my feet. 'If
you do not wish to speak to me, I shall not
ask again.'

I left the kitchen and began to count to
ten. I'd reached the magical seven when I
heard the patter of feet behind me. I turned.
Alicia stood there breathless.

I cupped her smooth cheek in the palm
of my hand. 'You have nothing to fear, little
one. I truly mean you no harm.'

'I wish to tell you the truth, sir.'

I guided her to a window seat. I peered through the thick and mullioned window at the gathering night.

'What is the truth, Alicia?'

'My mistress loves Sir Ralph.'

'That is evident. But was this love pure?'

'I don't — '

'Is your mistress an adulteress?'

She sat back, her face pale, biting her lip.

'You came to speak,' I said gently. 'Will you not do so?'

'My mistress is a good woman,' she said earnestly. 'She loves Sir Ralph passionately, more than life itself.'

'And he?'

'He is a fair knight.'

'Do you love him, Alicia?'

Her eyes fell away.

'Did your mistress and Sir Ralph share the same bed before Lord Gilbert died?'

'No!' Alicia's face was defiant. 'But they cared passionately for each other.'

'How do you know that?'

'How do you think I know?' she snapped. 'By look, word and sometimes even touch. Love is so obvious, Master Henry.'

'So, you know my name?'

She blushed. 'The whole castle is talking

about your arrival. When a woman is in love, Master Henry, deeply in love, she cannot hide it. Lady Joanna came alive, vibrant.'

'But passion must have its outlet.'

'Must it? In small ways perhaps. Gifts at Christmas and Easter. The way they talked and walked.'

'Where did they walk?'

'Here in the castle. In the gardens and orchards, sometimes down to the village but always in full view.'

'They were never caught alone, stealing away? You know the way life is in a castle, Alicia. People hide from each other.'

'The Lady Joanna hid nothing, nor did Sir Ralph. She was his lady, he was her knight.'

'And didn't Earl Gilbert object?'

'Earl Gilbert didn't care.'

'Do you know what happened in his Chamber of Shadows?'

'No.'

'What was the relationship between Earl Gilbert and the Lady Joanna?'

'It was like watching mime, Master Henry, where the players never speak or look at each other. That's what Earl Gilbert and Lady Joanna were like, mummers.'

'You are well schooled.'

'My father was a priest.' She smiled. 'I am

145

of bastard stock but he taught me to read and write. I know some Latin and a little French. That's how I gained employment here. After the Lady Joanna gave birth to her third child, her old maid retired because she became ill. I had served in one of Earl Gilbert's manor houses where I met the Lady Joanna on her travels. She liked me and asked for my companionship. I was only too happy to serve.'

'Did she and Earl Gilbert live as man and wife?'

'After the birth of the last child, not that I saw.'

'But that birth was years ago.'

Alicia shrugged and held her hands in her lap. I caught her glance before she lowered her eyes; Alicia was not the innocent she pretended. She had come here to tell me something and hoped that morsels of information would serve the purpose.

'Go on, Alicia,' I said. 'I need more than hints and innuendo.'

She raised her head. 'The Earl Gilbert was a violent man. On a number of occasions he would visit Lady Joanna's bed, it would be late at night. I am not too sure what happened there but . . . '

'But what, Alicia?'

'One night I heard raised voices. I came

146

out of my chamber and listened at the door, not because I was being a curiosity seeker — '

'Of course not,' I interjected.

'No, sir, I am not. I was alarmed for my mistress. In his cups Earl Gilbert could be violent. I heard my mistress say, 'Sir, if you harm me again, I swear I will kill you!' I became frightened so I ran away. I never heard my mistress speak like that, although she could be cold; indeed some of the servants called her the Lady of the Snows. The next morning she was her usual self but I sensed something was wrong. I confessed to my eavesdropping. Lady Joanna was dressed in her nightshift. Without a word she undid the cord and let it slip to her ankles. On her left side, just above the buttocks, was an inverted V. The wound was old and healed, the flesh puckered and pink.'

'And?'

'Lady Joanna picked up her shift and turned to the matters of the day. She did not need to explain, I recognised the mark of a branding iron.' Alicia saw the disbelief in my eyes. 'It's true,' she said. 'A princess of England treated like a common whore or strumpet. My mistress never talked about it again. Once I tried to ask but she pressed her finger against my lips, tears brimming in her eyes. Of course, the other servants talked. I heard rumours about violent quarrels, screams — this was from the early years of the marriage — but no one dared mention it openly.'

'But the screaming continued didn't it, Alicia?'

'A different sort. During the day when he was sober, Earl Gilbert was a good lord, a hard man but with some dignity. When his belly was full of claret, the prudent kept out of his way. Fortunately he usually closeted himself in the Chamber of Shadows. There were whispers, gossip about him having terrible nightmares.'

'Did you hear his torment?'

'One night I was disturbed by footsteps and shouts. The next morning the talk was that Earl Gilbert's sleep had been plagued by phantasms but what they were, no one would say. I asked the Lady Joanna but she just shrugged and looked sadly at me.'

'And the night he died?'

Alicia became agitated. 'I've heard the rumours,' she said softly, 'but nothing was said openly before the Lady Joanna was taken by her father.'

'And what are these rumours?'

'That Earl Gilbert was pushed to his death.'

'Was he?'

'God knows, Master Henry, but I tell you this, the Lady Joanna could not have had a hand in it. I was with her in her chamber. We were going through robes for the winter when the messenger came. My lady threw her cloak round her and we hastened to the east tower. When we reached the steps to the Chamber of Shadows, Ralph Monthermer was there, together with Tibault and Ricaud.' Her lip curled at the mention of these two names.

'You do not like them.'

'No, I don't, and they don't like me or my mistress. They are the source of the whispers.'

'Why don't they like the Lady Joanna?'

She narrowed her eyes. 'I don't really know. My lady would have nothing to do with the seneschal. 'Let him get on with his business,' she would snap. As for the priest, Lady Joanna barely tolerated him anywhere near her. She described him as a snake in the grass.'

'Tell me about Earl Gilbert's corpse.'

'It lay at the foot of the steps, the neck awry, a pool of blood spreading out. My lady asked who was with the Earl. Tibault murmured something I did not catch. My lady was pale, disturbed, but she made no pretence at grief she did not feel, and that was her manner throughout the mourning period.'

'What do you believe caused Earl Gilbert's death?'

'I think he tripped. Only later did the rumours begin that he might have been pushed.'

'But not by his wife. She was with you.'

'I will swear it on the Holy Bible, if you wish, Master Henry, and other servants saw us hurrying through the castle. She couldn't possibly have been there.'

'Did you notice anything strange?'

'Ricaud wished to examine the corpse but my lady was most insistent. There's no physician or leech nearby except Father Benedict, he's a Dominican preacher who serves the village church. In his former life he was a physician and an apothecary. My lady has a deep respect for him. Riders were despatched to fetch him. Father Benedict examined the corpse carefully.'

'What did he find?'

'The points of Earl Gilbert's hose were undone and his cloak had been tied wrongly. And when a guard was sent up the steps to check the Chamber of Shadows, he found the door unlocked and off the latch.'

'And what do you think that signifies?'

'That someone else was with the Earl. If

he was alone when he left his room, he would have locked the door and put the key in his wallet. Earl Gilbert was very careful about the security of his chamber.'

I felt a chill of fear. This young lady's information about an unlocked door and the disarray of the Earl's clothing was the first real evidence I had uncovered that the death might not have been an accident.

'I understand Sir Ralph found the corpse? Why should he be the one? I thought no one was allowed near that chamber?'

'They weren't. Sir Ralph was to meet the Earl at the foot of the steps where he would report on the preparations for the hunt the following day. After he was knighted, Sir Ralph became Earl Gilbert's principal squire.'

'Some people here in the castle must have objected to that. Weren't their noses put out of joint?'

'I can't comment on that, sir, but Sir Ralph was intensely disliked by Tibault and Ricaud.'

I turned and pressed my hand against the cold mullioned glass. Tibault and Ricaud again. Were they antagonistic towards everyone in the castle? Why?

'What was the attitude between your mistress and Sir Ralph as they stood at the bottom of the steps?'

'They hardly looked at each other.'

'You are keen-witted and sharp-eared, lass. Have you discovered if anyone else was with Earl Gilbert that night?' When Alicia hesitated to answer, I added, 'You have heard the rumours about the Lady Joanna. If the accusation of murder can be laid at her door, it can always be laid at another's.'

'There were visitors,' she said guardedly.

'What visitors?'

'I don't know, sir. I can't say more.'

Alicia became so tight-lipped I wondered if she was telling me the truth, but clearly there was no point in pursuing the matter then.

'Did Ricaud the priest give absolution the night Earl Gilbert died?'

'Father Ricaud blessed the corpse which was taken to the Earl's bedchamber and dressed for burial. A requiem Mass was sung in the village chapel by Father Benedict. Again, the Lady Joanna was most insistent and, before you ask, Father Ricaud did not like that.'

'And after the funeral?'

'Lady Joanna dressed in widow's weeds.'

'Did her relationship with Sir Ralph change after the funeral?'

Alicia sighed and got to her feet. 'Death doesn't stop love, Master Henry.'

'No,' I agreed, 'it doesn't. But you know that wasn't what I was asking.'

Alicia leaned down, her pretty face earnest. 'As God is my witness, the Lady Joanna and Sir Ralph committed no sin!'

I don't know whether she had told me the truth before, but I had no doubt she was telling the truth now.

'Goodnight sir.'

'Goodnight,' I replied. 'And may the courts of Heaven bless you.'

She disappeared back into the kitchens. I took out my rosary and thumbed them for a while. I don't know whether I was praying or calming my mind. Are they one and the same thing? I took a cresset torch and continued my tour of the now dark and lonely castle. A sleepy-faced servant led me to Sir Ralph's chamber. It had been stripped bare. When a man falls from grace, it is wonderful how quickly his possessions disappear. Not one scrap, not one article of clothing remained. It was a soldier's chamber. A black wooden crucifix hung on the wall. There was a cot bed, a table, chairs and stools, chests and coffers, all of which were empty. The window was narrow and overlooked the fields to the south of the castle. I saw a prick of light among the trees and wondered if it was some itinerant traveller or a peasant out poaching.

I put the torch in an iron bracket and sat with my back to the door.

'If I was Sir Ralph?' I murmured. 'And I was in love with this castle's lady, I'd be sharp enough to know that walls have ears and eyes.' I paused. 'No doubt,' I continued talking to myself, 'if I had some midnight tryst with my lady, my chamber would be watched and so would hers.' Yes, I reflected, that would be the case. But so far I had been unable to plumb the depths of their relationship. It is certainly passionate, the sort of love which makes the heart sing and the blood thrill.

Suddenly tears came to my eyes. For some reason this business swept me back down the years to Oxford. It was as if the ghost of Crispin, with his merry mouth and laughing eyes, joined me in that chamber, dancing with the other shadows as he used to dance so expertly in the taproom of the Blue Boar tavern — before love put an end to it all!

I shook my head and wiped my eyes. The passion between Monthermer and Lady Joanna must have had some expression, I thought. I had found one poem; could I find another? Or a letter? Or some keepsake? The bed drew my eyes. I walked over, pulled it away from the wall and, crouching on my knees, felt the floorboards but they were

154

nailed securely. The wall was white-washed, hard brick covered by a thick white paste. I ran my fingers over it. I could detect no crack. I pushed the bed back, lay down on it and stared again. My eyes searched every inch of the wall in front of me. Then I saw it; one brick protruded slightly. I got up and pulled at it. The brick came away smoothly; there was no crumbling of the plaster around it.

'This,' I murmured, 'was craftily done with great patience.'

The brick was ridged on all sides, which concealed any form of disturbance when it was in place. I thrust my hand into the cavity and felt a small roll of parchment. I drew it out. It was tied with a piece of red twine. I replaced the brick, took the torch and returned to my chamber. The castle was now silent except for the occasional howl of a dog or the neigh of a horse from the stables. I undid the piece of parchment and smiled. The love poem, written in a hand I did not recognise, reads as follows:

If Love turns
It cuts
Like a blade seeking blood.
We are blades, not blunted,
Every turn, we cut and bleed.

We seek release
But keep on turning
And turning, cut and slash.
Love bleeds,
It drains,
It finishes.

Love is like a light,
Snuffed out.
And the blackened room hungers for
   change.
Love's light goes
But the fragrance remains,
The silver shards,
Rays of light.
A heart breaks
And, in so doing,
Shatters worlds.
Yet no one hears.
The dark is all around
Love's light leaving its mark.

Love lost like
Love found
Nothing.
Love-ache from an
Empty heart,
Nothing.
Love calls love and
Finds

Nothing.
Love's God, God's love
But nothing.
Love for itself, naked,
All things.

The writing is bold, that of a clerk, not Sir Ralph's, and certainly not the Lady Joanna's, or Earl Gilbert's — not that he had the soul or wit to write a poem such as this. So who else was involved? And why had Monthermer kept the poem, and hidden it?

The candle began to gutter, a sign that the day's work was done. I changed for bed, said my prayers and fell asleep. I dreamt of things that might have been rather than what they were. I woke late the next morning. I had not left orders to be roused so I shaved myself quickly, washed and dressed. I pattered a swift Ave in the chapel and went down to the great hall where food and drink were still being served. It was deserted, only scrounging dogs nosing among the rushes for scraps, though some children came in to play at skittles. I decided to stay there. If people wished to speak to me, they would come.

I watched the door to the kitchens to the right of the dais and, sure enough, a fish swam into sight — Tibault the seneschal, dressed in a grey woollen gown edged with blue, which fell down to the knee of his brown leggings. His boots were mud-spattered, his cloak still about his shoulders. Full of his own self-importance, with his hand on his belt which bore jangling keys and two heavy purses. Clearly, he had been performing his duties as seneschal, inspecting the barns and granges. He stood for a while sipping wine as if he hadn't noticed me. When he did, he showed mild surprise and strolled over. He is a narrow-faced, flint-eyed stalk of a man, with a bulging Adam's apple in his scrawny throat and thinning black hair. His sharp eyes would never miss a duty owed or a tax unpaid.

He sat down opposite me. 'Good morrow!' He scratched his chin.

I did not like his false, fox-like voice, nor those hooded eyes.

'I thought you would see me first, Master Henry.'

'If you thought that,' I replied, 'you could have come to see me. I have not concealed myself.'

'I am very busy.' He put his cup down.

'We have that in common, sir.' I pushed away the platter of salty bacon and rye bread. 'Since you are a busy man, Master Tibault, I will not waste your time. You didn't like the

Lady Joanna, did you? More to the point, she never liked you. Did you exchange pleasant words with Sir Ralph?'

The man was startled by my brusqueness but, God forgive me, I didn't like him or his type. Here is a man, I thought, full of petty hate who would dance the jig if Sir Ralph's neck was stretched at Tyburn.

'I found the Lady Joanna difficult,' he replied. 'And Sir Ralph, well, he was Welsh.'

'So was my mother,' I lied. 'How does it matter, Tibault, what a man is?'

'He was an upstart, a newcomer.' His face had turned a choleric red and I was reminded of the old Gaelic prayer, 'Oh God, make my opponents arrogant.' People full of pride and pomposity can easily be stung into letting their tongues run ahead of their wit.

'Now, why is that, sir? Sir Ralph was Earl Gilbert's favourite squire, knighted by the King.'

'Quite so, quite so,' came the terse reply.

'So, I am correct. You did not like the Lady Joanna or Sir Ralph.'

He swallowed hard and nodded.

I got to my feet. 'I wish to see the Earl's Chamber of Shadows and you have keys. Come.'

He seemed surprised but led me out of the hall, across the courtyard and up into the east tower of the keep. The Chamber of Shadows was on the second floor; a winding, spiral staircase led to it. The masons had carved the staircase into the wall of the keep but it was badly drained; the walls were mildewed and damp, and pools of water glinted on the cracked flagstones. The door at the top was black and forbidding, reinforced with iron studs. I noticed there were two locks, strong and well-oiled, built into the door, not the type that can be taken off.

'It was Earl Gilbert's wish,' Tibault explained, noticing my interest. 'He hired the best locksmith in London to make them — Clavering. He lives near St Mary Axe opposite the Priory of St Helen.'

I knew Clavering by name and reputation, the Exchequer and Chancery often hired him to build coffers and caskets.

Tibault unlocked the door and it swung open.

Every chamber has a soul, every dwelling place an emanation, and the Chamber of Shadows lived up to its name. It was a gloomy, menacing place. It prompted thoughts of ghosts, goblins and sprites, of witches on haunted moors and she-wolves hunting in the mists. It stirred memories of childhood nightmares about scaly monsters and dark, bottomless pits. The stone walls were hidden behind wooden screens joined together in the form of an octagon which swept up to meet a ribbed and vaulted ceiling. There were no windows, no corners, no crevices where any demon or twilight folk might hide.

As Tibault went about lighting the purple-edged candles, I stared round in amazement. I noticed a small vent in the roof. Tibault, when he had finished his task, followed my gaze.

'Behind the wood,' he said, 'are windows and vents, for this is really a chamber within a chamber.'

The floor was painted black as was the table in the centre of the room and the high-backed chair with its purple cushions. A human skull was on one side, papers on the other. A tray bearing quills and pumice stone, a sharpener, sand for documents and pieces of red wax lay in the centre. A few books and an almanac stood next to them but, apart from these, the chamber had little to show. I noticed the shelf on one of the walls was clear and glimpsed a stain on the floor near the table where a tripod stood hidden beneath a cloth. Above the door hung a crucifix. I went and took this down. Something else had hung there and been recently covered with the cross. I walked back to Tibault and thrust the crucifix into his hand.

'This is a warlock's chamber,' I said. 'I could take you into certain parts of London, Master Tibault, and show you rooms with the same octagonal shape, the same dark colour, the lack of religious objects.'

'But the crucifix!'

I ignored that. 'All that's missing here are the purple drapes, books of spells and curses, jars.' I pointed to the table. 'And a cloth bearing the signs of the zodiac. This room has been cleared hasn't it? And why is the air so sweet?' I asked. I had noticed the scent as soon as I entered the chamber. 'This place has quite obviously been purged and perfumed, and a crucifix hung on the wall for good measure. You knew I was coming. On whose orders was it done?'

'On mine.'

Ricaud the priest, dressed in a dark woollen cloak, stood in the doorway. Short, black, cropped hair framed a pallid face, close-set eyes, and bloodless lips. He looked like a man who would not be frightened easily. He carried his rosary as if it was a weapon rather than a religious object.

He looked me up and down. 'I am priest of this castle, Master Henry. I decided it should be cleared. I had the magic books, philtres, potions, jars, hemlock and mandrake all burnt in the midden yard.'

I sat down in the high-backed chair. 'On whose authority?'

Ricaud kicked the door shut and walked across.

'The authority of the Holy Mother Church.'

I almost smiled at his quick reply. The look in his eye challenged me to argue the point. But I know the Codex Juris Canonici, the canon law of the Church: anything tinged with black magic must be seized and burnt immediately. In this matter, there was no debate.

'Were you Earl Gilbert's spiritual comforter?' I asked. 'Did he come to you for confession? Did you shrive him and offer him absolution?'

'I tried to.'

'And did you warn the Earl that this nonsense,' I gestured to the room, 'is condemned by both Church and Crown?'

'I did but I had no power to make him follow it.' Ricaud faced me squarely. 'Earl Gilbert was a deeply troubled man.'

'That,' I replied, 'is apparent but the King did not know of it.'

'Very few people did.'

I gave a sigh. 'Father Ricaud, I carry the King's commission and, like you, I am a very busy man. I arrived in Tonbridge yesterday and I must be gone by tomorrow. You know why I am here.'

'You investigate the Lady Joanna's adultery with Sir Ralph Monthermer,' Ricaud answered quickly.

'You have proof of that?'

'Earl Gilbert suspected it.'

'Did he now? So he must have questioned the young knight.'

'Earl Gilbert had his pride.'

'Then he didn't? So, did he question his wife?'

'No.'

'But he talked to you about it?'

'Yes.'

You're lying, I thought. I studied his eyes; they were like little black holes. And you are full of hate. I have met priests like him before, filled with arrogance, hungry for power, quick to take offence.

'You did not like the Lady Joanna, did you?'

'She was headstrong. She found obedience to her husband difficult.'

'Obedience?' I queried.

'She refused to have him in her bed.'

'Because he was violent? Because he was impotent? Or was it both?'

I was pleased at the surprise in his face.

'I know a little bit more than you think, priest.'

Tibault had slunk away into the shadows. I now regarded him as a mere cipher; this priest was the source of the gossip and rumour against the Lady Joanna.

'Shall I tell you, Father Ricaud, what I know? Earl Gilbert was a violent man. Not for nothing was he called the Red Earl. He had been married before and his first wife managed to secure an annulment. The Lady Joanna soon found out why — Earl Gilbert abused women. He was tormented by demons. How could any true son of the Church build a chamber like this?' I chewed the corner of my lip and studied this snake in the grass. 'Do you know, Father Ricaud, what I am beginning to suspect?'

'What do you suspect?' came the sneering reply.

'I suspect that Earl Gilbert hated his wife so much that he tried to trap her in adultery. Oh, don't look so shocked, or so coy. Earl Gilbert liked young Ralph so he brought him back from Wales and in his demented rage at his own impotence he sought to use him to trap and shame the Lady Joanna.'

The priest looked down his nose at me as if I was some sinner come to be shriven.

'What you say,' he stuttered, 'is preposterous!'

'The truth often is, priest. Master Tibault,' I said sharply, 'come out of the shadows!' I leaned across the table. 'Can either of you produce one shred of evidence, one witness prepared to take the oath that Lady Joanna committed adultery with Sir Ralph?'

'Before Earl Gilbert's death, no,' Ricaud answered sharply. 'But afterwards, when she was in her widow's weeds, they would often go walking down to the village unaccompanied. Sometimes the servants found traces of leaves and bracken on the clothing of both our turtle doves.'

'And you take this as proof of adultery?'

'Why should they go walking alone in the woods?'

'You said they walked down to the village.'

'Oh, they'd go and see the hedge priest there but — '

'Father Benedict is no hedge priest,' I retorted. 'He is a man learned in physic. Perhaps our two turtle doves, as you call them, preferred his presence to yours. Once again I ask you, can you produce one shred of evidence — and I am not talking about smiles, touches or presents — that they were adulterous either before or after Gilbert's death?'

The priest glowered malevolently.

'Do you know of anyone who could

produce such evidence?'

'Our doves were cunning,' Ricaud protested.

'So the answer to my questions is no.' I undid the wallet of my belt, unrolled the royal commission and placed it on the table. I drew my dagger and placed it on top of it. 'You know what this is?' I tapped the bottom of the parchment with the tip of the dagger.

'A royal commission,' the priest sniffed.

'And that makes me a royal judge. Now, you can answer my questions here or before King's Bench in Westminster. Don't worry,' I offered false reassurance, 'I will make sure you have a comfortable chamber in the Tower. Of course it could take weeks . . . '

Ricaud glanced quickly at Tibault, who just shook his head.

'Very well.' I spread out my arms. 'Why did Earl Gilbert fashion a chamber like this? And don't play games with me.'

'Earl Gilbert had a bloody past,' Ricaud replied quickly. 'He could be a contentious man but he came to me asking for comfort. He said he was haunted by demons, the ghosts of men, women, children whom he'd slain.' The priest closed his eyes. 'He said they came to him at night, thronging round his bed, maimed and bloody. I tried to soothe his mind, quieten his humours, but it was

167

impossible. On two occasions he tried to tell me something. His lips would move but no words came out. He was like a man with the falling sickness. He could not sleep and he no longer lived as the husband of Lady Joanna.'

'So he turned to the black arts?'

'He looked for help.' Tibault stepped closer. 'He ordered me to bring him carpenters, men from villages along the Medway. He had this chamber fashioned. No one was allowed further than the threshold. When he journeyed to London, he always brought back books on the black arts.'

'And?' I glanced at the priest. 'Come, come, Father, if he could not find spiritual comfort through you, he must have turned to someone else.'

'There's an old woman,' Ricaud replied. 'Well, not so old. She calls herself Malherbes. Some call her a wise woman, others regard her as a witch. Earl Gilbert often visited her, and later he invited her into the castle. She always came after nightfall, cowled and cloaked. The Earl himself would meet her by the postern gate and, on the evenings she came, no guard was ever posted.'

'This woman should have been arrested!'

'We had no proof of black magic, no one knew what went on, the door was locked and

168

bolted. Afterwards, the woman left as quietly as she came.'

'But you knew when she came?'

'Oh yes. A castle is an enclosed community, gossip is tossed from tongue to tongue.'

'And the night Earl Gilbert died, was she here.'

'I think so.'

'Is it true that Earl Gilbert's clothing was in disarray and the door to this chamber was open on the night his corpse was found?'

Tibault nodded.

'Yes,' Ricaud agreed.

'And isn't it also true,' I continued, not knowing whether it was or not, 'that one of you came up to this chamber shortly after Earl Gilbert died?'

The seneschal stepped back into the shadows and, for the first time, the priest was visibly shaken. There was a sudden looseness around the mouth, his eyes shifted, a quick wetting of dry lips, fingers moving as if he wished he had something to hold on to. He pulled a stool across and sat down.

'When you came up,' I asked, 'what was here?'

'The chamber was in darkness.' Ricaud stared at the wall. 'All the candles had gone out. The chamber was ice-cold, yet it was a fairly mild evening. It smelt like a midden-heap.'

'But you lit the candles, didn't you? You must have done, you are curious. You are a priest, and for the first time ever you were in the Chamber of Shadows.'

'Yes,' Ricaud nodded, moving restlessly. 'I was curious, more curious than fearful.' He swallowed hard. 'I had a tinder in my wallet, the same I used to light candles in the chapel. I could hear the people downstairs gathered round the corpse and their voices reassured me. I struck the tinder. I had great difficulty lighting the candles. It was as if their wicks resented the flame. My hand shook, I began to sweat and I called out, didn't I, Tibault?'

'Yes, yes, you did,' came the reply.

'What did you call out?' I asked.

'I don't know. Something to reassure myself.'

'And when the candles were lit?'

'I expected to discover something dreadful but all I found was a small goblet containing blood. I don't know where it came from. There was no animal corpse in the room, just this small earthenware pot, half-filled with blood. Later I took it downstairs and tossed both cup and contents down a latrine hole. It was curious, the bowl was warm to my touch.

I picked up one of the candles and looked around at manuscripts, open books, various objects which have now been burnt.' He paused. 'I am almost certain someone else was here. I had a feeling of being watched — it wasn't pleasant.' Ricaud shuddered.

'I became frightened,' Ricaud continued. 'I took the cup, left the candles burning and came downstairs. A few days later, Lady Joanna held a meeting of the principal officers of the castle to announce her plans for Earl Gilbert's funeral. She asked about the Chamber of Shadows and I volunteered to clear it. This time I brought guards. The chamber seemed different, it smelt more like an outhouse, but the men were nervous.' Ricaud shrugged. 'We cleared it and that's how you find it now.'

'And Malherbes? Did Lady Joanna talk of her?'

'No. It was as if the woman never existed.'

'I thought it was a great kindness,' Tibault spoke up, coming forward. 'Lady Joanna could have sought her out and arrested her. There was enough gossip about her and witchcraft.'

I looked at this precious pair. 'Let's go back to the night of Earl Gilbert's death. He apparently left here in a hurry, stumbled on the stairs and fell to his death. Soon afterwards his corpse was found by Sir Ralph.'

'So he says.'

'And what do you say, Father Ricaud?'

The priest lifted a bony finger as if about to deliver a homily.

'I want to know what you think,' I insisted. 'And why.'

'Earl Gilbert may have slipped.' Ricaud sniffed. 'But there's a possibility, Master Clerk, that Monthermer came up here.'

'Why should he do that?'

'Perhaps he was summoned? Or he wished to confront the Earl?'

'Confront? Why should he confront? The Lady Joanna was Earl Gilbert's wife. Or,' I leaned across the table, 'was Earl Gilbert doing something to his wife which Monthermer objected to? Or did Monthermer believe that Earl Gilbert was allowing him a certain freedom with his wife?'

'All that's possible.' Ricaud smirked. 'In which case, Master Clerk, you are in agreement with me. Monthermer may well have come up those steps. A quarrel might have broken out. Sir Ralph is a brawny young man.'

'And you think he took Earl Gilbert, flung him down the steps, and when he realised his master was dead he proclaimed the news to the rest of the castle?' I pulled a face. 'I know that Earl Gilbert had demanded to see Sir Ralph. It was the general custom before the Earl retired, wasn't it?'

I pushed back the chair and stood up. Vague suspicions stirred but I did not want to share them with these two. 'I want all the screens and every other wooden item taken from this chamber and burnt within the day. Do you understand? Let every item be consumed by fire.' I nodded at both of them, left the chamber and walked down the steps.

I noticed that the top steps were firm and broad. There was nothing to cause a man to miss his footing. Did Ricaud have the truth of it? Had Sir Ralph's patience snapped?

Behind me I could hear Tibault and Ricaud in hushed conversation. They no longer interested me. They had provided some information but no clear answers. I walked out into the courtyard and for a while I just sat on the steps revelling in the sunlight and the ordinary sounds and smells of the castle. A greyhound came loping up and licked my face. The captain of my escort swaggered across, a jug of ale in his hand.

'Are we leaving, sir?'

I squinted up at him, shading my eyes against the sun. 'Have my horse saddled,

Captain. I am going to ride down into the village.'

'Alone?'

'No, Captain, with my thoughts.'

The man grinned and sauntered off, leaving me to my speculations. Why had Earl Gilbert kept Monthermer in the castle after it became obvious that his wife loved the man? Far from banishing his squire, the Earl had promoted him. Did he take some spiteful pleasure in watching his wife long for someone she couldn't have? Did he, as I had suggested to Ricaud, hope to trap the Lady Joanna and brand her as an adulteress? Or was he one of those twisted men who take illicit pleasure in watching an adulterous affair develop? Is that why he really wanted to meet Sir Ralph at the bottom of the steps to the Chamber of Shadows? Was he teasing the young knight? Did he like to know where he would be when darkness fell and would-be adulterers come into their own?

'Your horse is ready, sir.'

I got up, grasped the reins and swung myself into the saddle. I was so lost in my thoughts, I was clattering across the drawbridge before I was really aware of it. The white trackway winding down to the village stretched before me, on either side high hedgerows where birds squabbled.

Now and again the spring breeze would carry the sounds of the labourers tending the soil and the shouts of their sons, armed with slings, driving away the marauding crows. I suddenly realised that in my preoccupation I had left the castle with no idea where Malherbes lived.

I reached the crossroads. Two chapmen, their donkeys hobbled, were sharing their food with a young boy from the fields; the wandering tinkers were trying to find out from him who lived where and the best place to sell. I offered the boy a penny; he forgot about the chapmen and showed me which lane led to the village. I asked about Malherbes.

'Oh, the witch lives some distance along there,' he told me, pointing at a trackway which cut off to the right and wound through a small copse.

'Is she a witch?' I asked.

The boy shrugged. 'Sometimes she is, sometimes she isn't. When all is well, she isn't; when things go wrong she is. People haven't made up their minds yet, that's what my father says.' And then he scampered off.

I urged my horse forward into the copse. It was colder here; the trees clustered together, branches interlocking, blocking the sky. I crossed a small brook, passed

175

through a clearing and entered a second one. Malherbes' cottage stood in its own grounds surrounded by a small fence. I could see herb plots and a small vegetable garden. I smiled to myself. Stories about the filthy hovels and gloomy dwellings of witches and warlocks did not apply here. The cottage was probably once a forester's house. Its stone walls had been freshly white-washed, the roof was neatly thatched, the shutters on either side of the door were open and the air was fragrant with cooking smells. A cat sunned itself on the stone steps. I dismounted, led my horse forward, hobbled it and went to the gate.

'You can come in, Henry Trokelowe.' The voice was firm and clear. 'I promise I won't change you into a toad — at least not yet!'

I walked up the well-kept path and noticed that the garden was neatly hoed. Fluttering scraps of rag strung across the vegetable garden kept the birds away. I entered a room which was stone-flagged, and had a fire burning in the hearth on the far wall. The woman was sitting at a table, cutting up some plant and placing the pieces into different pots. I gazed around. At the far end, reached by a ladder, was a bed loft. Onions and other vegetables hung from the rafters, next to a piece of ham and a chunk of salted pork. A tidy, neat place. A crucifix was fixed on the wall, as well as pieces of embroidered cloth to add a little colour. There were even rugs on the floor.

'Surprised, are you, clerk?' The woman looked up and, with her wrist, pushed the greying hair from her face. 'Take your cloak off, sit by the fire.'

'You are Malherbes?' I asked, unhitching the clasps of my cloak.

'That's my present name but I was baptised Juliana.' She rose and stepped closer into the light.

She was tall and pleasant-featured, with light-green eyes in a strong face. The cheeks were deeply furrowed, as if she suffered some inner pain and anguish. Her greying hair was parted down the middle. She was dressed like a nun in a grey gown clasped at the neck by a brooch shaped in the form of a snake. Thick, heavy sandals were on her feet. Her hands were clean, her nails cut, and on her marriage finger she wore a silver circlet.

'What did you expect, Master Henry? Some hook-nosed harridan murmuring curses over a boiling cauldron?'

'I did not know what to expect,' I replied, 'though you obviously expected me.'

She chuckled deep in her throat and gestured at one of the box chairs before the fire. 'It was not through the black arts! All of Tonbridge knows the King's clerk, Henry Trokelowe, is here. So, when I see a well-dressed clerk on an even better fed horse, ah, says I, here is Master Henry. And you would have to come here. If Hinkley didn't tell you about me, Alicia would; if Alicia didn't, Tibault would; and if Tibault didn't, Ricaud certainly would.' She sat down opposite, took an earthenware jug from the grate and filled a pewter stoup.

'I brew it myself,' she said. 'Don't worry, there is no root of mandrake in it.' She filled a cup for herself. 'So, let me have a look at the King's clerk. Past his thirtieth year, dark-brown hair, long face and clean-shaven. Innocent green eyes which stare unblinkingly. A controlled, neat man who takes good care of his teeth and his hands. Not a mark of food on your jerkin or hose. So, what will you do, Master Henry? Threaten me? Send messengers to the Sheriff of Kent? I have done business with him so I don't think he will be too happy. Or are you thinking of dragging me to London?'

I leaned back in the chair and sipped from the cup; its taste was fresh and strong.

'You chatter, mistress. Like a squirrel on a branch.'

'I want to save you time, Master Clerk.

Ask your questions then go. I'll tell the truth.' She shrugged one shoulder. 'What is it to me?' Her green eyes shifted, she put the cup down. The cat leaped into her lap. It sat there, a deep purr in its throat as she scratched between its ears.

'You could be accused of witchcraft.'

'Perhaps, but could I be condemned?'

'There are those in the castle who know of your nocturnal visits to the Red Earl in the Chamber of Shadows.'

'That does not prove black magic or the demonic arts.'

'Why did you go there?'

She smiled at me. 'Hinkley says you are an honest man with a mind like a hungry ferret.'

'You keep yourself well-informed, mistress.'

'Let me tell you my story.' She looked into the fire. 'Of course, my real name is not Malherbes. I was born of good yeoman stock in the King's shire of Somerset. I was raised at the baptismal font and named Juliana Cuttlesfoot. My father had five daughters, marriage dowries were expensive so I was sent to the nearest nunnery as a novice. I fell in love with a wandering minstrel. No, no, not one of your ragged-arsed urchins, a real minstrel, a Frenchman from Provence.' She smiled. 'He had a face like an angel

179

and a kiss you'd never forget. He stayed in our guest house for three days and, when he left, I went with him. The poor Abbess nearly died of fright, my family disowned me. I married the minstrel. We wandered the highways and byways. I had his child. We reached one of the Cinque Ports, Rye or Winchelsea, I forget which. Here both my husband and little boy died. It's a terrible life, Master Clerk! When you fall, there's no one to catch you. I sold myself, I became a sailor's whore till I caught the eye of a nice, plump merchant. I became his concubine, living in a little chamber in an alleyway off Cornhill in London, that's where I met Draxford.'

I must admit, the cup nearly slipped from my hand.

'Draxford the Augustinian priest?'

'No, Master Trokelowe, Draxford the former Augustinian priest, who became a warlock, a dabbler in the black arts. I became his disciple in more ways than one. He was a very good magician but even worse than the merchant in bed. He taught me everything he knew and I taught him all I had learnt. We were a precious pair. Draxford, as you know, liked to surround himself with comely damsels, his 'little tray of sweetmeats' he called us. Then he had to go and poison a rival. So the Sheriff's men took him and he was fried alive in Smithfield.'

'I remember it,' I said. 'I was one of the King's witnesses. The place reeked of human fat for days afterwards. His screams were terrible. They should have killed him before the fire was lit.'

'Draxford died as he had lived, hideously. It was no more than he deserved, Master Henry.'

'And you, mistress?'

'I took to wandering once again, but this time with a lighter heart. Draxford was dead and my demons had gone with him. Eventually I joined a company of truly wise women who knew the properties of different herbs, and from them I learned the art of good physic. Then I came here.'

'And met de Clare.'

She nodded. 'The Red Earl paid me a visit. He knew of my past and demanded my help; if I did not give it, he would see me hanged.'

'What did he need help for?'

'He wanted peace.' Malherbes leaned across and pressed her fingers against my forehead. 'His mind was a chamber filled with ghosts.'

'We all have ghosts.'

'Not like de Clare's,' said Malherbes.

181

'Thirty years ago civil war raged in England. De Clare was entrusted with the task of suppressing the London rebels. In the course of his duties with the gibbet, the axe, and the sword, he came across a group of Jews — three or four dozen of the unfortunates. They, like any sensible person, were fleeing from the riffler bands in London. De Clare's soldiers caught up with them. They were innocent of any crime but de Clare's blood lust was insatiable. He herded them into a barn, sealed the doors, then burnt it to the ground.' She refilled her cup. 'And they call me a witch!' She offered me the jug but I shook my head.

'An old man escaped. He cursed de Clare in his own tongue and said that not a day would go by but he would be tormented by the Jews' deaths. De Clare cut him to the ground with his sword.'

'And the ghosts came.'

'They did indeed, like wraiths through a mist. At first de Clare only heard them, voices murmuring in corners, sudden screams and shouts. Then he began to see them. He'd be hunting and he'd glimpse them clustered beneath a tree; in the dining hall they would watch him eat; when he lay down to sleep, there they would be, in a corner of his bedchamber. Even in church they would

182

watch him from the choir loft.'

Her words rang true and I felt myself go cold.

'At first they were indeterminate shapes; as I said, like someone glimpsed through a mist. As the years passed, they became more distinct, and they increased in number. De Clare had an iron will but eventually their constant presence poisoned his soul and destroyed his life. How could any man love a woman, love his children or love himself when the ghosts of those he had slaughtered constantly thronged about him? It affected Earl Gilbert's mind and the power of his groin.'

'So it is true, he became impotent,' I said.

'Yes. De Clare, who prided himself on being a stallion, became no better than a gelding. Being a man of little faith, he could not turn to religion so he turned to me.'

'And you helped him through the black arts?'

'No, Master Henry. I tried to help him with potions, philtres and incantations.' She gripped my knee. 'I used to massage his privy parts with ointments and unguents.'

'Why did he hate the Lady Joanna?'

'He didn't hate her. It was in his nature to abuse women, all the more so when he could do nothing to satisfy his lust.'

'Did you ever meet the Lady Joanna?'

'Indeed I did,' said Malherbes. 'Lady Joanna came here before the Earl ever did.'

'What for?'

'Potions to induce sleep.'

'Did you gave her them?'

'I gave her crushed camomile to soothe the nerves but she came back for stronger potions, some of which could cause eternal sleep.' Malherbes scratched the cat's head. 'I never really made up my mind whether she wanted it for herself or her husband.'

'What about Monthermer?'

'Ah, now there was a lusty one. He needed no potions from me to mount and ride the Red Earl's wife!'

'They were playing the two-backed beast before the Earl's death?'

'The Red Earl believed it.'

'Did you?' I asked.

'Before his death, I cannot say, but after he died I saw it with my own eyes. Early in the summer of the following year, I went out to gather herbs. In the forest, Master Clerk, it is wise to move silently. I learnt to do that long ago, and not just in the forest; it has its uses in the city as well. Anyway, I reached the edge of Grayscott Clearing, deep in the woods.' She smiled. 'Lady Joanna and Sir

Ralph were there, naked as the day they were born, locked in passionate embrace.' She paused. 'It was beautiful. Whatever they may have done, those two loved each other. I know, because I, too, have loved like that, with my husband, Geraldus.' She looked at me sharply. 'Some people say love is a sickness, Master Henry. It isn't, not in the sense of a malady. It is a hunger, a deep hunger for another person.'

So here was the witness I had demanded of Tibault and Ricaud the priest. And if Sir Ralph and Lady Joanna were lovers after Earl Gilbert's death, then why not before?

'The night Earl Gilbert died, were you in the castle?' I asked.

'I was and I left.'

'Why?'

'Earl Gilbert was demanding that I summon up a demon. He'd brought up the blood of a cock. He was wild-eyed with drink. He asked me to smear some fat on his body and make the necessary incantations. I was afraid.' She looked directly at me. 'Our world is like a pool of light; at its edge lies darkness. Those who venture too close to the darkness disturb its denizens and imperil their souls. So it was with Earl Gilbert. Yet I had no choice but to obey him. I took the chalice and, for the first time in many a year, I made

185

the secret incantations to call up the demon world. The room became icy cold. I felt my skin crawl. My nose caught a reeking stench as if something offensive had crawled into that chamber. I fled. I ran down those steps and out of that castle, vowing I'd never return.'

'Did Earl Gilbert follow?'

'No. I slammed the door shut. I met no one, except Sir Ralph who was crossing the courtyard.

'Did he challenge you?'

'No. He glanced at me and that was all. A typical soldier, Master Henry. I wasn't his business so he passed on.' Malherbes breathed in deeply. 'A day later I heard that the Red Earl was dead.'

'Do you think Earl Gilbert also fled from that chamber, tripped and fell?'

She shrugged. 'It's possible, though he seemed determined to stay. It was as if the torment of his mind allowed him no escape from whatever evil my words had summoned to the chamber. I can tell you no more, Master Henry.'

I thanked her for her time and for the ale and walked out into the sunshine. I was glad to be free of that cottage. Malherbes was comely enough, she posed no danger, yet there was about her a tinge of the night, a touch of darkness, that oppressed me. I unhobbled my horse and swung myself into the saddle.

It was now well past noon. As I urged my horse back along the trackway to the crossroads, the countryside lay quiet in the warmth of the sun. Only the occasional crashing in the thicket or some bird singing high in the green coolness broke the peace. The woods on either side were dappled shadows. At the crossroads I turned towards the village. The ale I'd drunk had made me feel sleepy and for a while I dozed, letting the horse have its head.

I reached the village and gathered my wits. On either side stood cottages of wood and stone, each surrounded by a fence with a plot of land before and behind. Pigs, dogs and chickens wandered about. Two children played with sticks and some of the village women sat in doorways, busy with sewing or simply enjoying the good weather. The menfolk were absent in the fields. I passed the tavern and saw the two pedlars I had met earlier, enjoying stoups of ale. They raised their hands and called me over. I smiled back but continued up the steep incline to where the Church of St John's stood on the top of the hill. The grey curtain wall of its graveyard hid long grass, bushes and yew trees, row upon row of wooden crosses and cracked, dusty tombstones. I left my horse at the lych gate and walked up the pebbled path. The main door was locked so I went round and entered through the corpse door at the side. The church smelt slightly damp and mildewed. It was small and rather gloomy, with squat round pillars and shadowy transepts but the paving stones were swept and the rood screen and altar rail were of well-polished oak. The nave was like any other, benches and stools stacked, baskets of flowers at the base of pillars. Candles glowed in the Lady Chapel to the left of the high altar; the chapel was much brighter, its walls covered with brilliant paintings.

'Can I help you?'

I whirled round. A priest had come out from the sanctuary. In one hand he held a candle, in the other a paring knife he was using to trim it. He was small and thickset with a cheery face under a mop of snow-white hair. He was dressed in the black and white robes of a Dominican.

'Are you Father Benedict?'

'I am,' he grinned, putting down the knife and wiping his hands on his robe. 'And you must be the royal clerk Henry Trokelowe. Would you like to come to my house? We can eat or drink.'

'No, thank you, Father, I have just visited Malherbes. Her ale is tasty but strong.'

The priest nodded and gestured that I should follow him as he turned to go back into the sanctuary. He stopped at the foot of the steps up to the high altar. I gazed around. The sanctuary was beautiful, its walls covered in paintings, their colours fresh and eye-catching. The small rose window was filled with painted glass, the pyx box was of the best silver while the altar was of the same polished oak as the rood screen. The steps were covered in a rug which had been pinned down. Candlesticks of the purest copper winked and dazzled in the light pouring through the rose window. It reminded me of St Olave's Priory.

'So you have been to see Malherbes,' said Father Benedict without turning his head. 'Now, there's a name to murmur in a holy place like this.' He went over to a side bench and sat down, inviting me to follow suit.

'What do you make of her, Father?' I asked.

'A sinner like all of us.' He smiled and his face became boyish. 'But a challenge for any Dominican.'

'Do you think she's a witch?'

'No, Master Henry, I don't. She's like you and me,' his bright brown eyes held mine, 'wounded, but in her the cuts go deep. In time God's grace will heal them.'

'Is that a Dominican or a physician speaking?'

'Both, learned clerk,' he answered. 'We priests are supposed to use Christ's power to heal men's souls. Does your soul need healing?'

'If I was what God wanted me to be,' I responded, quoting from the classics, 'then I would be a great saint, but because I am what I want to be, I am a great sinner.'

Father Benedict laughed and tapped me on the knee. 'Knowledge of yourself is the beginning of wisdom. Even royal clerks can be saved.'

'And royal princesses?'

He still smiled. 'I think the Lady Joanna will be saved.'

'What about Earl Gilbert?'

Father Benedict gestured with his thumb over his shoulder. 'The Red Earl lies buried in the side chapel. There's not much to see. The stonemason has yet to finish the effigy. I am not too sure whether he'll be saved. He's buried close enough to God but what matters is not where you're buried, but how you lived.'

'Some people say Lady Joanna and Sir Ralph might have committed adultery.'

'I might commit adultery,' said Father Benedict, then laughed to himself. 'No, that's a lie. I could try to commit adultery,' he patted his stomach, 'but it would be a case of the mind being strong and the flesh being weak.'

'Is the Lady Joanna an adulteress?' I asked directly.

'I am her confessor,' the priest replied. 'What she tells me in the confessional must remain with me. But it is no secret that she fell deeply in love with Sir Ralph. Before the death of her husband, however, she committed no sin, except perhaps in her thoughts but, like you and me, she's flesh and blood.'

'And afterwards?'

'I cannot tell you, clerk.'

'Well, I can tell you.' I was harsh and blunt, though God knows I shouldn't have been. As I described what Malherbes had seen in the woods, Father Benedict became agitated and avoided my gaze.

When I had finished he just nodded. 'All I can say, Master Henry, is that to the best of my knowledge the Lady Joanna committed no adultery.'

He got to his feet and stood over me. 'She is all that a princess of England should be and she adores her father but, beneath that, there's another Joanna. I wouldn't say she is a visionary or a mystic but I honestly believe that if the King put her on the highway in her shift with Ralph Monthermer beside her, she would think that she had won everything and lost nothing. In her the flame of love has always burnt brightly, and meeting Sir Ralph fanned it into a blaze of searing heat. I have met it before,' he smiled, 'in women more than in men. And do you know, I envy her. I wish I could love someone like she loves Sir Ralph. I wish I could love God as she loves her knight.' He paused, his fingers to his lips. 'Christ commanded that we should love our neighbour as we love ourself. Well, the Lady Joanna loves Sir Ralph more than herself. He is as much a part of her as her brain, her womb and the blood which beats in her heart.'

'Is it a sickness?' I asked.

Father Benedict laughed. 'Master Henry, I have read your commentary on Constantine the African's treatise on lovesickness. I must tell you honestly, I disagree with him and with your conclusions.'

(Your Grace, I was flattered and embarrassed. Here was a stranger who had read my work!)

'Why?' I asked.

'There's no such thing as lovesickness.

Well, not in my opinion. There's just love hunger.'

'But I don't feel hungry.'

'Don't you, Master Henry? Or are you like a monk who fasts and controls his hunger for other purposes?' He studied me closely. 'Yes, that's what you are, Master Henry. I think you have experienced that hunger and brought it firmly under control.' He shrugged. 'Please don't be offended. So have I. Some people fill that hunger with other things — riches, possessions or, sometimes, themselves, so that they have no room for anyone else.' He pointed to the side chapel. 'Or, like the Red Earl, they twist the hunger into a craving for something else.'

I went and looked at the stone tomb. It was nondescript, a square stone plinth, awaiting its effigy.

'I understand you inspected his corpse, Father.'

'Yes. I could find no trace of violence, except a broken neck and bruising caused by a fall down narrow stone steps.'

'They say his clothing was in disarray.'

Father Benedict scratched his chin. 'Then they, whoever they are, should ask what the Earl was doing in his pestilent chamber. God knows, I don't!'

I wandered into the Lady Chapel — its

paintings attracted me. I have always been fascinated by the vigour and skill of wandering artists whose work is to be found in churches. One painting in particular caught my eye. It was freshly done, of a man and a woman, each drawn in marvellous detail, solemn in expression, both garbed as courtiers though they had taken their shoes off. The woman was clothed in a blue and grey dress gathered at the neck, a simple girdle round the waist. She had the face and hair I have seen in the depiction of many a court scene. The man's features and hair were also unremarkable. He was garbed in a dark-green jerkin which fell to just above his knees, with hose of the same colour. Father Benedict, behind me, began to fidget, clinking the keys at his belt.

'Who did this?' I asked.

'Fabiani from Hainault. I understand he wanders the shires of southern England. He has skill, does he not?'

The wall had been carefully dressed for the painting and the colours used denoted considerable expense. This was not the work of some humble artisan but a court painter, a master artist, who would demand good coin for such splendid work.

'Who commissioned it?' I asked though I suspected the answer.

'The Lady Joanna. She favoured our church. It was finished last autumn.'

I took one of the large candles from the side altar, lit it and studied the painting more closely. The man and woman are standing in a bedroom. The chamber is sumptuously furnished with red and blue rugs, a wooden chest by the half-open window. The bed is a four-poster, the woodwork intricately carved, its curtains of the costliest taffeta. Over their heads hangs an elaborate candelabra. A small terrier stands between them, head up, tail erect. The man (and I am sure it was meant to be Sir Ralph) has his right hand raised as if taking an oath and with his left he holds the lady's hand. I am certain, Your Grace, that she depicts your daughter the Lady Joanna. The colours are rich but soft. The candelabra, strangely enough, bears only one candle and it is lit, even though it is apparent the scene takes place in daylight. On the far wall hangs a mirror; it reflects two shadowy figures, certainly not the man and woman who dominate the scene. Round the mirror eight roundels depict the Passion of Christ. The back of the chair next to the bed is surmounted by a carving of a lady kneeling at prayer, a huge dragon rearing above her. I recognised the scene from the life of St Margaret. On the wall to the left

195

of the mirror hangs a rosary, and to the right a dusting brush. The artist has placed some fruit on the windowsill, apples and plums, and on a chest are three peaches and a bowl of pears. Paintings like these always intrigue me, the scenes within scenes they show and the symbolism they contain.

I blew out the candle and gave it back to Father Benedict who had now lost some of his ebullience.

'Why did the Lady Joanna have this done?'

'As I told you, Master Henry, it was a gift to the church.'

'But why that particular scene?'

'I believe it's something from the classics. Lady Joanna never really explained.'

'No, no, of course she wouldn't,' I murmured. 'Father Benedict, do you have anything else to tell me?'

His eyes went back to the painting and then quickly looked away.

'What will happen to them?' he asked anxiously. 'Will the Lady Joanna come back here?'

'That is for the King to decide,' I replied. 'The allegations against the Lady Joanna and Sir Ralph are that they not only committed adultery but murder also.'

'That's a lie,' Father Benedict retorted, and

then quickly recovered his humour. 'Unlike adultery, I could certainly commit murder, and if you met some of my parishioners, you'd understand why.'

'For all our sakes, Father, and particularly theirs, I hope it is a lie.'

I bade him adieu and returned to the castle where I received your message. I am glad Your Grace has agreed that your daughter and Sir Ralph may write to each other. It distracts them and, although they can use a cipher, that can be broken. I did not delay my departure but packed my belongings, collected my escort and left for St Wilfred's Priory on the outskirts of Bristol. My scribe Winborne will be there and, as Your Grace knows, there's not a cipher Winborne cannot break or a seal he is unable to loosen.

I dictate these final words in a tavern on the main Bristol road and after careful reflection I would advise you not to use guile and deceit against Sir Ralph. This rarely leads to the truth and is scarcely just. I shall see Sir Ralph myself at Bristol and, by Your Grace's leave, decide on appropriate action in dealing with both Sir Ralph and the Lady Joanna.

Written and sealed at the Silver Griffin tavern, the feast of St Verontius, May 1297.

Letter 6

From Ralph Monthermer to Lady Joanna, Princess of England and queen of my heart, health and greetings.

I will surely die if I cannot lie in your arms again. I am incomplete, not whole. My hunger for you grows. What will come of this?

You called me your falcon, your hawk, but I am pinioned fast, all I see are strips of sky and flashes of the sun. I am kept close and constantly watched. Now that I have read your letter, I am resolved on escape. I shall cut myself free or die in the attempt. I am a knight, a warrior. I have been imprisoned and face no charges except that I love you and you love me. Is that a crime? Is it treason? Where does it say in Scripture, the teaching of the Church or the laws of England that a certain man can only love a certain lady?

I have no doubt that although the seal may appear unbroken and our cipher is known only to us, your father will use these letters to his own advantage. This only adds to the burden of each day that I spend apart from you. It might be months before my kinspeople in Wales discover where I am, and even then what can they do? I cannot tolerate this confinement, week in, week out. I love you. It's not my loss of freedom but separation from you that cuts the deepest.

I have stopped to read your letter again. Now I know all that has happened. Do not feel guilty at telling your father the truth. Better it come from you than someone else. I have no regard for the likes of Tibault and Ricaud or your husband's witch woman; it was only a matter of time before fingers were pointed and allegations made. I laughed to myself. When I was first taken, I feared that your strength would give out or your heart would fail. More silk than steel. Now I know different. In Palestine the Saracens swathe themselves in silk which is a better protection against the cutting sword than the finest steel. You are my silk, my cloth of gold. You have withstood the onslaughts of your father. I do not fear the torturers or the clever questions, or even death, but I could not endure separation for life.

Stay strong. Whatever the powers of Hell, or your father, throw against us, I am resolved to be free. Thick walls, swords, spears and the fastest pursuit cannot stop me. You will tell me to be careful but you must know in your heart of hearts that I cannot withstand this imprisonment. Memories can comfort: walks through the woods of Tonbridge, sitting in the nave of that old, dark church. Yet memories are only a fragrance not the substance, a mirror which supplies an image but not the reality.

We shall be one again. You will be safe, your children will be safe. Thank God they are still young and cannot fully understand the turbulence which surrounds our lives. You hide yourself well behind the chatter and gossip of the convent. You use it as I would a shield. I smile at that. One thing I have learned about women, and you in particular, is the way you turn the everyday things of life into a defence against its blinding cruelty.

The tedium of imprisonment stretches the days and prolongs the nights. I no longer go down to the exercise yard. If I am to die, to suffer some unfortunate accident, then let it be because I rebelled against your father, used all the powers of my heart, mind and soul to escape this prison and see you once again. I fret, I must break free. If I did I'd storm the convent and carry you off, defying both King and Church. The good Constable Sir Miles, or rather his spy at the peephole, appears to have sensed this. The number of guards in the corridor outside as well as in the courtyard below have been doubled. There are constant visitors to my cell. Sir Miles, the physician, servants — there's always an excuse. Now I have the lawyer Cordell. I am sure it is he who sits at the peephole. Perhaps that is the real cause of my agitation.

Cordell visited me again, with Sir Miles in attendance, to ask me the same questions. Am I an Adamite? Have I been married? Does he wish to weary me into admitting I am not the man I claim to be — the man you love? Are they trying to destroy me in your eyes? I am a soldier, I have fought in France, on the Scottish march and in Wales. I have confessed to you that, before we met, I was no saint.

This time Cordell brought parchment, quill, ink. He made himself comfortable at my table. Outside in the corridor I could hear other voices, including a woman's.

'You are Ralph Monthermer?' Cordell began.

'I am,' I replied, 'and I want no more of your childish prattle.'

He lifted his sly face. 'If you refuse to answer, the record will read that you agree with what I ask. Are you an Adamite?'

'I am not.'

'You know what they are?'

'Heretics,' I replied. 'They include a few priests, even lawyers. They believe that Adam and Eve, because they lived in the natural state, were pleasing to God.'

'How do you know about them?'

'How do you?'

'Sir Ralph,' the Constable intervened. 'I beg you to answer these questions. Master Cordell is here at the King's order.'

'Why should I answer? If I am on trial, where are my accusers?'

'You have taken an oath of fealty to the King!' the notary snapped. 'You must answer these questions. Now, tell me what you know of the Adamites.'

'The Adamites were powerful and widespread in Normandy,' I replied wearily. 'They secured a foothold in Wales. My parish priest, Father Ambrose ap Howell, was accused of being a member of the Adamites. He often preached there was no need for the sacrament of marriage.'

'And did you support him?'

'Father Ambrose is a distant kinsman. When the Bishop of Llandaff investigated, he sent men to seize him. Matters got a little out of hand. I and others intervened.'

'Because he was an Adamite?'

'No, because he was a good priest and

my kinsman. True, he had madcap notions. Sometimes his wits wandered but he loved and cared for his people. He lived a holy and austere life, a true servant of God. Do you know what that is, notary?'

'Have you lived a lecherous life?'

'Who with?'

'You are well known to the young women in and around your manor.'

'So?'

The notary sniffed. 'You campaigned in France?'

'I did campaign in France. I also served in Lord Mortimer's retinue on an embassy to Paris.'

'And you know the Roi des Ribaudes?'

'Who doesn't?' I retorted. 'He is king of the pimps and manages the brothels in the Rue Julienne.'

'Did you go there?'

'That's my own business.'

Cordell balanced the quill between his fingers. 'I do not believe you are some perfect, gentle knight.'

'I never claimed to be.'

'You have a reputation with the ladies. Have you no wife in Wales?'

'Not that I know of,' I laughed. The look on Cordell's face sobered me. 'Why, are you saying that I do?'

'Enough of this play-acting!' Cordell looked over his shoulder at Sir Miles. 'Bring her and the hedge priest in.'

The two figures who came into my cell meant nothing to me, I swear. The priest was scruffy, his lined face ingrained with dirt, with cunning eyes and mean lips. His grey hair was tousled and thick with grease. The robe was new; I wager Cordell had bought it for him. The wench was vaguely familiar: tall, raven-haired, a full if not fat face, pretty in a sharp, bitchy way with shifty eyes and pouting mouth.

'Do you recognise these two?'

I shook my head. 'The wench possibly, not the priest.'

The woman looked down at me and smiled.

'But sir, I am your true and loyal wife.' Her voice was sing-song, the words clipped. 'We exchanged vows before Father David here.'

'Where?'

'On the banks of the Severn, beneath a shady oak tree, six, seven summers ago. You pursued me but I would not let you have your way. So you bought a ring from a chapman, and we sought out Father David.'

'I remember it well,' the priest grinned. 'Hot and lecherous you were.'

I glanced at Sir Miles. 'Is this the best you can do, sir?'

'Are you calling me a liar?' the woman shrilled.

'What is your name?'

'Margaret, Margaret Shalford.'

My memory stirred. I remembered an escort, a convoy of carts taking munitions to one of the King's castles. We stopped at a tavern and remained there for three or four days while axles were repaired and greased, new wheels fitted.

'You are a tavern wench,' I replied. 'We may have tumbled in the straw but married? Never!'

She clutched at her gown and glanced at Cordell. 'You are my husband. I know your body. You have a scar running from your stomach to above your right thigh.'

I pointed to the spyhole in the wall. 'And how long have you been there?'

To give the doxy her due, she blushed slightly.

'How much have you been paid?' I asked.

'Paid?'

'Well, how did you know I was here? Were you and this priest both visiting the castle by chance and found that your long lost husband was in prison on the King's orders?'

'I made careful search and found them,' Cordell intervened. 'They are here at my request.'

'Will you go on oath?' I asked them.

'We will!' both chorused.

'Master Cordell, what is the penalty for perjury?'

He hesitated before answering, stroking his chin. 'Mutilation, branding.'

'And you are prepared to put both these people on oath?'

'I am,' he declared.

I glanced up at the woman. She was becoming nervous.

'You say we married six or seven summers ago. Which is it, six or seven?'

'I can't recall.'

'Why didn't you search for me?'

'I did not know where to look.'

I got up, kicked away the stool and pulled up my jerkin, displaying the scar. 'And you say you remember this scar because you are my wife and have lain naked with me.' I turned to the Constable. 'Sir Miles, take heed, you are witness to this.' I was now certain of my dates.

The Constable stared at me.

I sat down. 'Master Cordell, seven years ago I was campaigning in North Wales. I served with the King's levies around

Shrewsbury, hunting down the last of Llewellyn's rebels.'

'It must be six years,' the woman interrupted.

'Six years ago I was sent to the garrison on Anglesey. In the autumn I moved to Chepstow.'

The woman's fingers moved to her lips. 'I can produce witnesses who will swear to my story.'

'Then I will produce others,' I said. 'The principal one will be Master Gervase Talbot.'

'Who is he?' asked Cordell.

'A physician. He and the monks of Lilleshall Abbey in Shropshire will all swear on oath that my scar is only three years old.'

'It's all lies!' Cordell's hand was shaking.

The hedge priest and his accomplice were edging towards the door.

I sprang to my feet and held the stool by one of its legs.

'Now, Sir Ralph,' warned the Constable.

'Oh, for the love of God,' I snapped, 'get these varlets out of here. If the King is to trap me in a web of deceit, he'll need to do better than this!'

Cordell, too, leapt to his feet.

I pushed the stool nearer his face. 'You are a liar and a trickster!' I shouted at him.

'If you were a knight or even a gentleman, I'd demand satisfaction.'

Sir Miles was already opening the door, shouting for the guards. Cordell and his false witnesses were ushered out.

Sir Miles returned, shamed-faced with embarrassment. 'That was not my doing,' he said.

'I had thought the King above such clumsy and ill-prepared attempts to blacken my name.' I shook my head. 'He'll not try that again.'

'No, sir, he won't,' came the cool reply. 'Master Henry Trokelowe is a very different kettle of fish.'

When Sir Miles left, I went to the window and looked out at the wild roses which climb the tower wall.

Is that what your father intends? I wondered. To chip away at our love, slip in some canker which will slowly corrupt? In this he will not succeed, not with me and, I know, not with you.

I listened to the sounds of the men in the tourney yard, the clash of wooden sword and shield. The King would try this, the King would try that. Eventually he might do nothing and just leave me to rot, to while away my days with sweet thoughts of you until the passage of time edges them with bitterness.

I glimpsed a lark soaring up above the castle. I wished I could join its flight. To calm myself I became lost in memories but I found them too painful. Some occasions I can't bear to recall. I wish you were with child, that our love had some living bond which could not be dismissed or broken.

I paced up and down and wondered how long I could bear these pressed-in walls. How I would love to be free, reckless, chasing you up some windy hill, laughing in the sun, kissing in the lush grass. I remember you lying next to me in the woods outside Tonbridge; you were staring up at the branches of a tree.

'We will grow old, Ralph,' you murmured. 'The wind, the sun and the earth will remain but there will be a day when we are no more. All that is ours will be gone but life will go on, that sun will look down on other lovers exchanging kisses with burning lips.'

I plucked a wild flower. Do you remember? I tickled your nose and stroked your cheek with it.

'Who cares?' I replied. 'Heart of my heart, why fear death when we have Heaven now?'

You poked me in the stomach with a stick,

crying 'You are a poet with wanton ways, practised in sugared lines!'

I seized you, gripping your arms. I said we would tread life's wine press together and go rose-crowned into the darkness. You laughed and said what a brave thing to say, but then you cried, turned away and would not speak again. Did you know this was coming? You are more wise and astute in the ways of the world than I. I was like a child playing in the sun, unaware of the shadows lengthening all around us, oblivious of the approach of night. You once said that if I was away from you, time would ease my pain. Did you really believe that? The opposite is true. Time does not ease my pain but deepens it with short, sharp stabs till the soreness taints every drop of blood, every beat of the heart, every quickening thought. You were my cloak, you enveloped me, body and soul. You kept me warm and now I am cold. Sometimes, just to amuse myself, I take quill and parchment to draw your face but I can't, though I can picture it in my mind in every detail. I can recall every turn and twist of your lovely lips, the cast of your beautiful eyes. I have tried to write some poetry, a song to express my grief but I cannot. All I can say is that I love you with every breath and will do so for all eternity.

Two days have now passed since I picked up this quill and tried to express my thoughts. Long, hard days, like passageways beneath a dank fortress. After Cordell left, Sir Miles kept well away from me. Perhaps he was embarrassed by the notary's pathetic fumblings. I was left to my reflections.

Your father seems intent on using the law against me. Pinpricks of fear drove me from my torpor. I recalled how the King executed the Welsh princes, inflicting a barbaric death by hanging, drawing and quartering. He proclaimed that as their suzerain he had the right to inflict a traitor's death on all who were taken in rebellion. What point of law will he use against me? Murder? I warned you before I left Tonbridge that I had heard scurrilous whispers that the Earl's death was not an accident. Or will he try witchcraft? Perhaps he will attempt to prove that I am some warlock who spun magical dreams to trap you. Or that I am a coarse soldier who abducted and raped you. After Earl Gilbert's death I said that I did not wish to be the cause of worry to you.

'Worry, sir knight?' you teased. 'Am I some damsel in an ivory tower waiting for my gallant squire to ride along? I have been raped. I have been terrorised by demons. Worry does not worry me!' Your beautiful face became grave. You grasped me by the jerkin, pulling me close. 'Losing you worries me.'

We discussed so often what we should do and how we should do it. In the end, you proclaimed, 'I must be direct, I must seize the opportunity with my father, be blunt and honest.'

Oh, my lady of the blunt word and the sharp wit, I praise you for your bravery. Our love is now known and, as the Scripture says, 'You cannot light a candle and hide it beneath a bushel of wheat.' And so, last night, I tried to escape.

My cell is broad and cavernous, its door set in a shadowy recess. I am a soldier and know how soldiers become clumsy and forgetful when danger recedes. I do not curse or show violence so they have grown lackadaisical and predictable. When the servant brings in food, the guard always follows him in. So, last night, I closed the shutters, lit one candle and made up my bed as if I was lying there. The door opened as it always does, when the castle bells toll for the garrison to come to the evening meal. The guard followed the servant in and, in the blink of an eye, I had my arm around his neck and his dagger out of its sheath. God bless them, they were only farm boys, not your professional killers or hired mercenaries. I ripped one blanket, tied their hands and gagged their mouths. They didn't resist. The soldier, before I took his war belt, whispered, 'Good fortune!'

I seized his keys, locked them in and crept along the passageway. On reflection I was stupid and dull-witted. I had barely reached the bottom of the steps before I was stopped. It was that shifting time between day and night. A guard called out the challenge and I went running but the inner gate was closed and guarded. I turned, sword and dagger up. Oh, for a few fleeting seconds I felt alive, taller than the castle, braver than any warrior of legend. Soon I was surrounded by a wall of swords, hauberks and spears. Anxious faces looked at me from beneath conical helmets. If they had wanted to, they could have brought me down with an arrow but their orders are strict, I am not to be killed. They came in closer. I knocked aside their lances and they retreated.

'Good evening, Sir Ralph.'

The voice was calm but it carried. The soldiers parted and Sir Miles, followed by a cloaked and hooded figure, walked towards me. The stranger had a clever, smiling face with searching eyes and the look of a perplexed parent.

'What are you doing here, Sir Ralph?'

The man pulled back his hood to reveal hair freshly cropped. He held out a gloved hand. 'My name is Henry Trokelowe, clerk of the Royal Chapel. I have come to talk to you, Sir Ralph.'

'I could kill you,' I threatened. My words sounded childish. How could I kill a man who looked at me as if he genuinely wanted to sit me down and share a tankard?

'You are not going to kill anyone,' Trokelowe replied. 'You are a man of honour, not a cutter of flesh. A tonsured knight.' He pulled back his cloak. 'See, I carry no sword. I want to talk to you about the Lady Joanna.'

'Like Master Cordell?' I retorted.

Trokelowe held up his right hand as if taking an oath. 'All I am interested in is the truth.'

I handed him my sword and dagger. I went to push by but he grasped my shoulder, his face hard set.

'Don't do that again,' he whispered. 'An arrow in the throat is no cure for love. Sir Miles.' He turned to the Constable. 'Let Sir Ralph join us for supper.'

'He's to be kept in his cell,' the Constable objected.

'Let him join us for supper,' Trokelowe insisted. 'Give me your word, Sir Ralph, that you will not escape.'

I did so willingly enough.

Trokelowe linked his arm through mine and we walked through the gates and into the long hall built just inside the curtain wall. It was a pleasant relief and welcome change from the stone walls of my cell with its wooden panelling, colourful shields, hunting trophies and weapons fixed in the plaster above. Torches and candles had been lit at the far end above the dais. Sir Miles clearly wished to honour his important guest. The table was covered in coloured cloths and laid with the best pewter cups, traunchers and plates. The smells from the kitchens beyond made my mouth water. Sir Miles was joined by other officers of the garrison, including Bastogne.

The meal was a sumptuous affair: stews and soups, venison pies, pheasant specially prepared; beef and pork, sliced and cooked, well covered in sauces; dishes of parsley and other herbs. There was almond milk as well as delicious wine which, Sir Miles explained, had been taken from a French ship seized off the mouth of the Severn. A large pike was also served and Trokelowe regaled us with stories of his own fishing, the nature and habits of the pike.

'It is a true wolf of the river,' he

proclaimed. 'The pike is a wily foe and is more intelligent than his brother fishes.' He glanced quickly at me. 'But that can be said of all God's creatures, can't it?'

I did not understand his meaning but he was gracious enough. He soon charmed Sir Miles and the others with gossip from the court about the possibility of war in Gascony and the King's projected marriage with the sister of Philip of France. Sir Miles and the rest pressed him about the campaign in Scotland.

Trokelowe's face became grave. 'The King is intent on crushing Wallace the rebel leader and Purgatory will soon be packed with the souls of the dead.'

Never once did he mention the reason for his visit. I sat on his left and he always ensured my wine cup was full. Eventually I could no longer tolerate his silence on the very reason both of us were there so, when a fierce discussion broke out about horses, I leaned closer.

'Lady Joanna,' I whispered. 'How is she?'

Trokelowe's eyes twinkled. 'I wondered how long it would take you to ask me that. I'll answer you truthfully: I have not met her. You know more about how the Lady Joanna fares than I do. The King has allowed you to write, has he not? No, Sir Ralph, I fish in a different pond.'

'And what do you hope to catch?'

'Why, sir, as always, the truth!'

'The truth is that I love the Lady Joanna.'

'No, sir, the whole truth.' He put his cup down. 'How much do you love her? Why do you love her? When did you begin to love her?' He plucked a piece of meat from his plate, popped it into his mouth and wiped his hands carefully on the napkin he had brought to the feast. 'I have been to Tonbridge,' his voice was still low, 'and I have talked to many. I have learned this and I have learned that.' He paused. 'What did you hope to prove tonight by leaving your cell?'

'Nothing.' I closed my eyes and leaned back in the chair. 'I was trying to prove nothing.' I glanced sideways. 'A pike swims, a bird flies. Sir Ralph Monthermer tries to escape.'

'Let me tell you more about the pike.' Trokelowe grasped my arm and squeezed it, a warning that we were not to converse on the matter in hand.

Eventually I returned to my cell. The door slammed behind me, the key grated in the lock. I opened the shutters and let the night air cool my skin. All I could think about was the day in the woods outside Tonbridge when we became one in body and soul and drank the sweetest wine from each other's lips. My soul ached for you.

I agree with you that Trokelowe is different from other clerks, a hunter in the shadows, a man of patience and subtlety. He invited me to sup so he could watch and listen as if he was standing on the edge of some pool determined to catch the fish of his choice. I felt as if I had been weighed and measured, my worth assessed. Here was a man who would tease the truth out, ask a question, sift the answer and, a short while later, ask it again to see if there was any difference. I slept badly last night.

Trokelowe came into my cell this morning, charming and relaxed, greeting me as if I was an old comrade. He asked for wine, a plate of bread and meat and sat opposite me at my small table.

'You enjoyed the meal last night? Sir Miles is a genial host. He means you well.' Trokelowe smiled and popped a piece of bread into his mouth, chewing it carefully, then smiled with friendly eyes, scrutinising my face. 'There are many who secretly admire you, a man who dared to challenge the King. In fact, they envy you. Not every humble Welsh squire is able to win the heart of a princess of England. Do you feel proud of that, Sir Ralph?'

'I feel proud of nothing,' I replied carefully. 'I am what I am and I love whom I love. Why should that be a matter for pride?'

Trokelowe laughed and sipped his wine. 'Would you believe me if I said I like you?'

'No,' I replied. 'You are the King's clerk, his lawyer come to tease out the truth. Like or dislike plays no part.' I glanced at the spyhole high in the wall.

Trokelowe shook his head. 'I've ordered that to be sealed, and before I leave Bristol I shall have words with Master Cordell. There will be no more hedge priests and tavern wenches to give false witness.' He put down his cup and joined his hands together as if in prayer. 'I apologise for that. This is too important for such games.'

'Why is it important?' I asked.

He smiled and shook his head. 'Let us begin at the beginning. You are the son of Edmund and Agnes Monthermer, a manor lord of Wales, kinsman to the powerful Mortimer family. Your father, and his lord, supported our King in his war against Llewellyn. The soil on your father's manor was thin. You grew up, one child among many, with a great deal of pride but little food, eh, Sir Ralph?'

'My father was a soldier. A good man but cold. He sent me to Father Ambrose to study the hornbook and learn how to read and write.'

'Ah yes, Father Ambrose. A goodly man. According to gossip you had a sharp mind. There was even some chatter about the Halls of Oxford or Cambridge.'

'But, as you said, my father was poor.'

'And so you left home to become a page in this castle, a squire in that manor, and gained experience of military service.'

'What is the purpose of all this?' I asked.

'The philosopher Augustine of Hippo made the shrewd observation that we are the summation of all our experiences. I want to find what your experiences are.'

'Why? Because I fell in love with a princess?' I picked up my cup. 'Master Trokelowe, men and women have been falling in love with each other, irrespective of their rank or status, since Adam met Eve in Eden. Do you think you will find some sort of key to unlock the puzzle of my ailment or learn what potion might cure this fever?'

For the first time since I had met him, Trokelowe became disconcerted. He glanced away. After a moment he asked, 'Why did you fall in love with the Lady Joanna?'

'I was serving in Wales,' I almost shouted.

'Lord Mortimer brought me to the attention of Earl Gilbert. He took a liking to me. I returned to Tonbridge. I met the Lady Joanna and I fell in love with her.'

'Were you brought up on tales of chivalry?'

'Not in Wales,' I said. 'More the stories of heroes, of brave warriors who fought strange beasts.'

'So you lived in a world of men?'

'Yes.'

'Did that please you? I mean,' Trokelowe waved his hand airily, 'some men have a natural liking for other men. Sometimes it is expressed in illicit love.'

'Master Trokelowe, I am not of such a nature.'

'And there again,' Trokelowe scratched his head, 'other men have a love of women which stays with them all their lives. I want to find out, Sir Ralph, why you fell in love with a particular woman. I don't want any untruths.' He paused. 'Let me give you an example. Four hundred years ago the great Odo of Cluny described how a certain Hukbert of Sens was given over to the sin of luxury and the pursuit of sexual pleasure. Every night he consorted with his concubines and gave himself up to all forms of lustful delight.'

'A fortunate man,' I laughed.

'One night Hukbert, now an old man, saw two women standing by him and realised they were not his concubines but phantasms. So agitated did he become that he eventually took refuge in a church, but the church, too, was full of phantasms, among whom sat one as queen. She ordered the phantasms to seize Hukbert and whip him. He begged to be released from this nightmare but they seized him and whipped him until people outside the church could hear his terrible screams. When the phantasms had finished with him, Hukbert's mind was deranged. He fell into a mortal sickness. Physicians were unable to help until one discovered that, as a boy, Hukbert had been notorious for being salacious with young girls and his stepmother, a cruel woman, used to beat him soundly for every transgression.' Trokelowe smiled to himself.

'I read this story in a book by Constantine the African,' he explained. 'He studied why people fell in love and why certain individuals became sick, even deranged because of it. Constantine studied the case of Hukbert and drew the conclusion that, in Hukbert's childhood, sexual pleasure and pain were closely linked. Years later these two principles came back as phantasms, not only to haunt him, but eventually take his life.'

I stared speechlessly at this clerk. Of all the paths he wished to take never, in my wildest imagining, did I think he would take this one.

'I am not Hukbert,' I remonstrated.

'Aren't you?'

Trokelowe raised his eyebrows.

'In all of us there is a touch of Hukbert. You see, Sir Ralph, do you really love the Lady Joanna or is it something else? Do you aspire for her because, deep in your heart, you know you'll never have her?'

'I will,' I replied. 'Either her or death.'

'Why do you say that? Why do you go to such extremes? Why must it be the Lady Joanna or death? Why not the Lady Joanna or some other woman? Is it death you are really seeking, Sir Ralph? Not the love of your life?'

I understood the clerk's cunning. He was not saying I didn't love you: he was not saying I shouldn't, nor was he saying it was illicit or illegal, but just merely asking why? He was forcing me back on myself, like a swordsman being pushed into a corner. Trokelowe refilled my cup.

'Sir Ralph,' Trokelowe murmured, 'I just want to talk. Surely in the days, the weeks, you have spent in this cell, you have asked yourself why? After all, you are a personable young man, a brave warrior, a knight. Sir Miles speaks highly of you. At Tonbridge you were well liked, you could have made a good marriage, perhaps to a rich heiress. Instead of that you became involved with a widowed countess, daughter of the King of England.' Trokelowe rolled the wine cup between his hands. 'This was not some passing fancy or secret passion which might be satisfied behind closed doors. It became the talk of the castle. Then Earl Gilbert dies and Lady Joanna confesses her passion for you to her father. Was that your doing?'

'No,' I said sharply. 'Not once did I ever tell Lady Joanna to do this or to do that.'

'But why her?' Trokelowe persisted. 'Sir Ralph, you are Welsh. The King has subjugated and brought under his power the principality of Wales. Is this some sort of revenge? Do you wish to subjugate the King's daughter?'

I leaned across the table until my face was only a few inches from his. 'Withdraw that remark, clerk, or as God is my witness you will pay for it.'

Trokelowe bowed his head. 'I apologise,' he murmured. 'I simply wish to understand why.'

'How can I express to you what I

cannot really express to myself?' I said in exasperation.

'Then let me take another path. Let us say, for the sake of argument, that your feelings for the Lady Joanna were not reciprocated. What then? Would you have pursued her? Or would you have left Tonbridge, vowing never to see her again?'

'Master clerk, if you left this castle and, on the King's highway, met a nun who fell deeply in love with you and you with her, what would you do?'

He laughed. 'I don't know. It's never happened so I can't comment.' He shrugged one shoulder elegantly. 'But I take your point. You cannot describe your actions in a situation that has never arisen.'

'All I can tell you,' I said, 'is that I fell deeply in love with the Lady Joanna. I don't know what was cause or what was effect. I don't know whether she loved me first and I responded, or whether I began it and drew her in.'

'You don't truly believe either of those possibilities, do you?'

'No, Master Clerk, I don't. Love is like a tinder being struck; the striking and the flame occur at the same time. You can't separate one from the other. I loved her and she loved me. And because she loved me, I loved her even more.' I waved my hands. 'This is not some problem you can divide into the beginning, middle and end.'

Trokelowe was watching me intently. His eyes grew brighter as I spoke, as if having turned the problem over and over in his subtle mind, he now believed he could glimpse a solution.

'Very well, Sir Ralph.' He drew an imaginary line down the middle of the table with his finger and placed his hands on either side of it. 'There was a time when you did not love the Lady Joanna and there was a time when you did. You crossed that line. Agreed?'

He could tell from my face that I did.

'Good.' Trokelowe drew back the sleeves of his jerkin. He seemed to have forgotten why he was here. He appeared genuinely interested in what I said, not as a lawyer or the King's clerk, but almost as if he was learning something which would be of benefit to himself.

'You seem to be enjoying this, clerk.' The words came blurting out before I could stop them.

He smiled at me; all cunning had disappeared from his eyes and face. 'Sir Ralph, I wish you'd call me Henry, Master Henry or Master Trokelowe. True, I am the

King's man, a royal clerk, but I was chosen for this task because I have a deep interest in what you say.'

'Why?'

He waved a finger playfully at me.

'One day you can question me, But,' he said sharply, like a schoolmaster eager to press on, 'let us return to the problem. We could talk about what you felt before, and what you felt after, but what was it that made you fall so deeply in love?'

My mind went back to that courtyard. Earl Gilbert dismounting, the shouts of his retinue, boots squelching in mud, horses neighing, sweat and breath rising in the cold air. Servants hurrying about and your face so strikingly beautiful, the cast of your eyes.

'It was her face. I had never seen anyone so beautiful.'

'Oh, surely, the Lady Joanna is a beautiful woman but — '

'No, Master Henry, for me she was the only beautiful woman. The look in her eyes caught my heart. I could have stood and stared until the sky cracked and Christ and his angels came again. I just wanted to stare. She noticed me and smiled, not with her lips, but her eyes.'

'And?'

'The Lady Joanna was like a wine I had

thirsted for all my life. I wanted to drink, drink and drink.'

'But before this moment, you were happy, were you not? You'd lain with women, you'd teased and flirted. So what was the difference?'

I thought of those first few weeks at Tonbridge, not because I really wanted to answer his questions, more to satisfy myself. I glanced up and caught sight of the crucifix, and I recalled something Father Ambrose had said about love.

'My love for the Lady Joanna is threefold,' I answered — and oh, heart of hearts, lover of my soul, this is the truth. 'The time before I met her was the time of waiting. The time of meeting was that of fulfilment . . . '

'And the time after?'

'Was of completion. It was as if my life was meant for her and hers for me.'

'What do you mean by completion?'

'I was not a moonstruck youth or lecherous in my thoughts. Her face, like a candle flame in a dark room, caught and filled my gaze. I felt in harmony.'

Trokelowe lifted his head.

'Yes, that's what I felt, that's what I mean by complete. Harmony with myself as well as with the world around me. It wasn't just happiness, it was a peace, a lasting peace, a feeling of being whole.'

'And her?'

'I cannot speak for the Lady Joanna. I will not speak for her. You asked me, Master Henry, how I felt. I have told you.'

'And how do you feel about her now that you are imprisoned?'

'The same. I compared the Lady Joanna to a wine and I must drink of it again. I said I felt at peace with her. Without that peace, without her, I do not want to live.'

I suddenly wondered what would have happened if you had not felt the same. I could not answer the question when Trokelowe asked it, and I am not sure I can answer it now. Perhaps I would have left, put as much distance between you and me as possible, ridden to the ends of the earth, fought the great Cham of Tartary or taken service with the knights who guard the frozen seas in the north. It would have been a living death.

'Have you ever loved like this before?' Trokelowe asked.

'Never.'

'What are your symptoms?'

'Symptoms?' I laughed. 'Master Henry, I am not ill, I am in love. If my heart beats faster and my blood pounds heavier that's because the Lady Joanna is music to my heart. Any ill effects I suffer are not caused by the Lady Joanna but by His Grace who has taken away my life, my love, and locked me in this strict and narrow place.'

'I have the power,' said Trokelowe, 'to provide you with lands and wealth, on condition that you always stay at least twenty miles from the Lady Joanna.'

'A terrible price to pay for such a short distance, Master Clerk. Tell His Grace I do not want his treasure, his manor or his lands. I want his daughter.'

'And if you are taken to one of the southern ports and banished from the kingdom, never to return, on pain of death? What then?'

'Then in truth, clerk, the King should kill me now because I shall return. No sea, no mountain, no river, no castle walls, no phalanx of armoured knights can keep me from my heart's desire.'

'And what if the King were to put you on trial for treason?' Trokelowe's face was grave. 'After all, Lady Joanna is a princess of England.'

I hid my fear of such a prospect but I could now detect the King's will in this matter. He wanted to be done with me; the purpose of Trokelowe's visit was to decide on the means.

'If the King has me put to death, he shall

answer for it to God as well as to his daughter. I will instruct my lawyer to etch on my gravestone in some dank and gloomy church: 'Here lies Sir Ralph Monthermer, knight, killed for love by his King.' '

Trokelowe smiled. 'Come now, Sir Ralph, that is somewhat dramatic.'

'It is the truth.'

Trokelowe got up and stretched. He seemed uneasy. By the rood, I thought, this man is not happy in his task. This is no Cordell eager to tie me up in a tangle of lies without a second thought.

Trokelowe walked to the door and stared through the iron grille. 'Tell me something, knight of the lovelorn, you say you've never loved like this before. Have you ever come close? No,' he lifted a hand but didn't turn round. 'Don't answer quickly, as is your wont, but think. Please, just think first!'

I closed my eyes and did so. A memory came to me, springing up from my youth, after I had left my home and a father who was stern, mercurial in his temperament, and more involved with his own thoughts than his brood of children. And Mother? Ice-cold, distant, very much the lady, conscious of her Mortimer blood and a genealogy which stretched back over the mists of time. I was thirteen, a page in some manor, and a serving wench took me into the stables. This was not some merry tumble, I was too young. She just sat, studied my face and held my hand. I felt a fleeting moment of true happiness but then it was gone.

I told Trokelowe. He tapped his fingers against the iron grille in the door.

'And tell me, Sir Ralph,' he said, 'have you ever witnessed love like yours or do you think you are the only one who seethes with passion and bays at the ice-cold moon?'

I ignored the sarcasm in his voice. 'Once, yes, I did meet love that was stronger than life itself,' I answered.

Trokelowe came back and sat down opposite me again. 'I was campaigning with the Lord Mortimer. He'd chased some rebels up some narrow fog-bound valley — they had attacked an outpost and plundered provisions. I took a group of horsemen up into the trees. We caught a man and gave him a choice: he could lead us to the nearest rebel village or we would hang him.'

I paused at the memory. You have changed me, Joanna. I could not do that now. I could not take a man and watch the fear blaze in his eyes. For how do I know such a man does not love like I do? How do I know that the death of such a man could not cause terrible pain to someone like you?

'The man agreed to guide us,' I continued. 'He led us along trackways we would never have found. We came to a small village, nothing much, a collection of cottages grouped round an old church. They must have known we were coming for they had fled. My men wished to burn the place but I told them not to touch anything, and I let the prisoner go.

'I drew my sword and walked up the pathway to the church. It was built of wood, with a simple nave and entrance tower. Inside, it smelt of wood smoke rather than incense. It had some benches and an altar, a huge wooden table. Everything precious had been removed. On the edge of the sanctuary was a carved lectern, shaped in the form of a soaring eagle. I have always admired such craftsmanship so I stopped to study it more closely. I was pleased that the church was empty, the villagers had fled, no blood had been spilt. I was about to leave when I heard a sound beneath me. I barred the door of the church and, coming back, pulled the lectern away.

The trap door beneath was small. I pulled it up and found a man and woman crouching below. I thought it might be the priest and his leman. He looked narrow-faced and nervous, certainly not a soldier. She was grasping him by the arm. They had been caught unawares and, unable to flee in time, were hiding in that hole. The woman glared at me fiercely and spoke rapidly. I could not understand her. I put my sword away and smiled. She spoke more slowly. My knowledge of the Welsh tongue is slight enough but I took her meaning. 'If you are going to kill us,' she pleaded, 'please let us die together.'

I glanced at Trokelowe.

'It wasn't so much what she said, Master Clerk, but the passion in her voice, the begging in her eyes. I had never met that before. She wasn't frightened of death, I could see that. She was more frightened of living alone.'

'And what did you do?'

'I dropped a coin into the hold. And a piece of cheese in a linen cloth from my pouch. I replaced the trap door and pushed the lectern back. I realised there must be another entrance. Perhaps somewhere in the cemetery there were secret passageways where more people were lurking. Now, my Lord Mortimer would have been very pleased to have caught a gaggle of rebels in one fell swoop but I couldn't forget that woman's face and voice.'

'What did you do?'

'I walked out of the church and told my men we were wasting our time. I left that village and its inhabitants.'

'Did you feel virtuous?'

'No, Master Henry, I felt sad.'

'Sad?'

'Yes, sad and envious. I had never met love like that before. I'd seen people beg for their lives but never beg to die with someone. For weeks afterwards I had a wild urge to ride back to that village, seek out the woman and ask her why. I lost all appetite for war. When the Red Earl invited me to join his retinue and leave Wales, I was only too pleased to accept. There are no rebels in Tonbridge!'

Trokelowe breathed in and tapped his cheeks with his hands. 'And when you came to Tonbridge, before the Earl's death, how did you and the Lady Joanna converse?'

'Why, sir, with our tongues.'

'You know what I mean.'

'Yes, Master Henry, I do. Lovers can say good morrow to each other and those two words can have a wealth of meaning. We talked about the ordinary things of life. Isn't it strange? We both knew what we were really talking about. I just wanted to be close to her; that was sufficient.'

'But you could see her marriage with your

lord was not happy.'

'Yes, though the Lady Joanna never fully discussed the matter with me.'

'Did the Earl?'

'Master Henry, what do you think?'

He did not bother to answer. 'You must have thought it strange.'

'It is common courtesy, and part of the knight's code, to pay court to the lady of one's lord. The Earl was a pragmatic man. At first I thought he approved of such flattery. Some men do.'

'But later on?'

'I became more cautious. The Earl was friendly enough but I would catch him watching me. I did not like it so I became even more prudent with the Lady Joanna. I sometimes wondered whether he wanted me to seduce his wife and was deliberately throwing us together. One evening, when I was in the apple orchard with Lady Joanna, I hinted at this. She pressed a finger to my lips, bidding me to keep silent.'

'And after the Earl died?'

(Joanna, I remembered our vow. I knew the moment had come.)

'I cannot and shall not answer that.'

'Why not?'

'You may be the King's clerk, Master Henry, but you are not my confessor. I will answer to a priest of my choice but not to you.'

Trokelowe dipped his finger into the wine and drew a line along the table. 'So, Sir Ralph, once again we have a dividing line, between the time before the Red Earl's death and the time after it, but you will not tell me what happened after it.'

'I will not. You may ask your questions. I shall not reply.'

'Then let us say,' Trokclowe tapped the line he had drawn, 'let us say Earl Gilbert's death had not occurred.'

'Master Henry, this is Bristol Castle, not the schools of Oxford. I cannot debate on what might have been or how many angels can sit on a pin or whether rainbows pour from rivers in the sky.'

'No,' he sighed. 'But let's tease the problem further. What would have happened if the Earl had not died? And please don't protest about speculation. You must have talked about this if you love each other so much.'

I decided to tell the truth, even though it meant admitting to a previous lie.

'Around the feast of the Assumption,' I declared, 'in the August before Earl Gilbert died, I did make a confession to Lady Joanna. I told her I loved her more than my own life.'

'Where did this occur?'

'Lady Joanna wanted to travel down to see Father Benedict. Earl Gilbert told me to accompany her. Usually she took her maid but she was ill with some distemper. The day was beautiful, a golden sun in a clear blue sky. All of nature seemed to be singing God's glory. At the crossroads I grasped the reins of her horse and confessed my love in a burst of words. She looked at me strangely: 'I feel the same, Sir Ralph,' she replied and pressed my cheek with the tips of her fingers.

'What can we do?' I asked.

' 'For the moment nothing,' she replied, 'but if God gives me strength, I shall petition Rome for an annulment.' '

Trokelowe seemed surprised. 'An annulment? On what grounds?'

'Lady Joanna refused to talk further about it, though I knew her husband was a cruel man.'

(My love, I did not think it just, or seemly, to tell Trokelowe, or anyone else, what you had told me in confidence.)

'Will you meet the Lady Joanna?' I asked Trokelowe.

He cupped his face in his hands and looked down at the table. 'No. A friend of mine, a Franciscan from Greyfriars, Roger of Evesham, he will question the Lady Joanna.'

'And then?' I asked.

'I don't know.' Trokelowe's hands fell away. He jabbed at a wine stain on the table. 'I have one more matter to discuss with you — Earl Gilbert's death. I won't play Hodman's Bluff with you. I have been to Tonbridge; the whispers grow stronger. You are held responsible for Earl Gilbert's death.'

So, we are come to the chitter-chatter in Tonbridge at last, I thought.

'You did find the corpse,' Trokelowe pointed out.

'And that makes me a murderer?'

'Why should Earl Gilbert fall down steps he knew well and leave his chamber door unlocked? He always secured it behind him. Some people say you went up there, became involved in an argument over the Lady Joanna and threw him down the steps.'

'On that evening, Earl Gilbert ordered me to come to the door of the Chamber of Shadows before I retired so that he could give me specific instructions for the following morning's hunt. At the foot of the steps I found Earl Gilbert. You've been to Tonbridge, you know the rest.'

'What proof do you have that you did not go up those steps and accost Earl Gilbert in his chamber?'

239

'Earl Gilbert always carried a dagger. If I had so much as attempted to put a foot inside that room, he would have drawn it. He was choleric in temperament and secretive about what happened there. If we had quarrelled, someone would have heard his raised voice. Earl Gilbert was a warrior. Do you think he would have let me just grasp him and throw him down the steps? That he wouldn't strike back? Clutch at me? He bore no other marks on his corpse. His dagger was not drawn. Earl Gilbert would not have died without inflicting some wound, mark or bruise on me. The Red Earl was as free with his hands as he was with his oaths.'

Trokelowe pushed the stool away and got to his feet. He studied the crucifix fastened to the wall. 'And you have nothing else to say?'

'Nothing except that I love the Lady Joanna more than life itself. I will not bargain or trade that love like some huckster in the market place. I have done no wrong to her or the Earl Gilbert. I am prepared to accept exile if the Lady Joanna is allowed to come with me. If the King wishes to send me into eternal darkness, I shall not go quietly, Master Henry.'

Trokelowe turned, fingers to his lips. 'No, I don't believe you will,' he murmured. He stretched out his hand and I clasped it. 'Think kind thoughts, Sir Ralph. I wish you well.'

It's hours since Trokelowe left. I lay down on my bed and stared at the bleak stone wall. I closed my eyes and saw your sweet face. I whispered words of endearment but they cannot truly express what my heart, soul and mind feel. I love you, Joanna of England, I always have and I always will. If we are not to meet again, then remember what you mean to me. No power on earth, or beyond, can change that.

Written at Bristol, the feast of St Theodosius, May 1297.

Letter 7

From Lady Joanna, Princess of England, Countess of Gloucester, to Ralph Monthermer, king of her heart.

Deepest love, if my fingers could only touch you! If my arms could embrace you then I would feel whole again. I have not heard from you. I have begun this letter and perhaps, before it is finished, I will be blessed with one from you.

I feel crushed by two millstones which grind my mind and soul into dust — the pain of our separation and the tedium of convent life. One morning it proved too much. I could tolerate it no longer.

I was in the herb garden plucking out weeds and turning the soil over. The convent was quiet, one of those short spans in the day when no bells ring or sandalled feet patter along stone passageways. A butterfly came and rested on a wild flower growing through the low wall built round the herb plot. Small and delicate, it rose, carried by the breeze, and moved across the grass towards the trees which ring the convent. By some strange fancy I thought it was a messenger from you.

So, holding the hoe in my hand as a pilgrim would his staff, I followed the butterfly and entered the trees.

The birds sang and I saw a rabbit feeding under the protection of a bush. Suddenly it froze. I crouched and waited, then it scampered away. I wondered how easy it would be for me to do the same. I followed the narrow path and came to one of the small postern gates in the wall that encloses the convent grounds. I took off my garden apron and, with the handle of the hoe, prised the rusty bolts back.

The trackway outside was silent. It was so easy. Swinging on the hoe, I strode down the lane. I felt free, like a girl released from the most onerous chores. I confess to doing a small dance and began to sing one of those songs I would for you: a French carol about true love unrequited. God knows where I was going or what I intended but the further I walked, the more vigorous I became. I was free. I would reach a village. I would do something. Bristol was not far away and I laughed at the thought.

Only then did I hear a footfall behind me. I whirled round and realised I had a retinue — six of my father's master bowmen, garbed in their green quilted jerkins, long bows slung over their shoulders, quivers of arrows at their sides. The captain looked embarrassed. He took off his helmet, bowed and ground his heel in the muddy trackway.

'How long have you been following me?' I asked.

'My lady, from the moment you left the gate.'

'And how long would you have let me walk?'

The man's nut-brown face broke into a grin. 'Until you decided to return. We are here to ensure your safety. My lady,' he continued in a rush, 'you are in open countryside. Outlaws, men of violence, are known to attack travellers, particularly a woman on her own.'

I banged the hoe on the ground as if it was a sceptre.

The man cleared his throat nervously. 'My lady,' he pleaded, 'I beg you. You may obtain your freedom but His Grace the King would have my head.'

I felt sorry for him. 'How many are there of you?' I asked.

'The convent is ringed by at least three hundred bowmen and men-at-arms are quartered in the villages around. Our orders are simple. You are not to leave here and no one may approach the convent without our permission.'

'Very well, Captain.' I opened my purse, took out a silver coin, and tossed it to him. He caught it deftly. 'I enjoyed my morning walk.' I walked by him and grinned. 'And, if you don't tell my father, neither will I.'

They escorted me back to the convent. I felt refreshed, more light-hearted. For a short while I had flown free of the cage. I knew what it was to be at liberty. I walked back to the herb garden and found Sister Agnes sitting on a turf bank, a small basket in her lap, which she was filling with marjoram and rosemary.

'It's for the kitchen,' she explained. 'Where have you been?'

'I followed a butterfly.'

The tired old eyes twinkled as she leaned forward. 'You're not becoming fey in your wits, my lady? It does happen here. We had one lady,' she giggled, 'a true madcap. She refused to wear her clothes.'

'That must have been a sight for the Abbess,' I replied.

I thought of the guards outside and studied this wrinkled old nun. I crouched down beside her. 'What are you really doing here, mother? Are you the Lady Abbess's spy?'

Sister Agnes's eyes brimmed with tears. 'I like to be with you,' she said. 'You have the life still within you.'

'What life?' I asked.

'You love and are loved.' She wiped one eye with a bony finger. 'That's what Veronica and I say. It is as if you are wearing a perfume. You know what perfume does, don't you?'

I stared at her.

'Certain scents,' Sister Agnes explained, 'can in a trice take you back years and memories come flooding back. You are in love and suffering because of that, while Veronica and I, all we have are memories.'

'And what is your advice, mother?' I asked.

'Never give up,' she said immediately. 'Never relinquish it.' She beat her little fists on the brim of the basket. 'That's what I say to you. And, yes, the Lady Abbess has asked us to spy on you.' She smiled impishly. 'But what we see and what we tell are two different things.' She edged closer. 'Sometimes at night I lie in my bed and feel I have my lover deep inside me. Does that shock you? An old woman thinking about the time she turned and took the love-kiss?' She got up. 'Come, I want to show you something.'

Intrigued, I followed her across the grounds into the chapel. We went through the haze of incense and into the choir. Sister Agnes took her seat in the stalls and gestured that I sit beside her where Sister Veronica usually sat.

'I'm going to tell you my secret,' she whispered. 'What do you see?'

I gazed at the stalls opposite. Their hinged seats were up, revealing the misericord beneath. In the wall was a half-moon shaped window of painted glass. It showed the mounted St George fighting the dragon which curled and snarled beneath the horse's dancing hooves. The knight, helmet off, was dressed in plate armour. His lance was lowered, aimed at the dragon's mouth. In the far distance, the princess he had come to rescue stood bound to a post. I could make out her green dress and long flowing hair. It was a typical scene, found in any Book of Hours and on the windows and walls of many a parish church.

Sister Agnes was staring at it. Her face seemed younger, the eyes more fresh, the lips fuller. She was talking to herself, lips silently moving, eyes fixed on that window as if she was seeing a vision.

'What is it?' I asked.

She blinked and smiled. 'When I came here,' she said, 'I brought a small dowry. I gave it to the Lady Abbess who, of course, handed it to the bankers. She asked me what

I wished to have done with the money. I replied I would like a painted glass window showing St George killing the dragon and rescuing the princess.' Sister Agnes's eyes were now full of mischief. 'The Lady Abbess hired a painter, a master glazier. The work was done here and because it was my window . . . ' She stared back up at it.

'That's you,' I laughed.

'Shush!' She put a finger to her lips.

I studied the painting. The more I looked, the more individual the features of both St George and the dragon's intended victim became. Indeed, I noticed other little additions. The dragon was wearing buskins or sabots which I had seen on the feet of the Lady Abbess. The face of St George was also original. Usually he has a bland face, with gold-blond hair framed by a silver halo. This St George had hair as russet as a squirrel's fur, rather slanted eyes, a full generous mouth and his face was cleanshaven. I marvelled at the cunning of the old nun, who could sit all day in church and stare at this faithful representation of her long-dead lover.

'The Lady Abbess must never know,' Sister Agnes murmured. She looked at me. 'She would be furious if you told her.'

I sat back in the stall and laughed until I had to cover my mouth with my hands. Sister

Agnes continued to gaze at the window, as if ravished by a vision. Softly she began to sing a rather ambiguous love song:

> I have a gentle cock,
> It crows at me all day.
> He makes me rise early,
> My matins for to say.
> I have a gentle cock,
> With a comb well set,
> Its feathers are of coral,
> Its tail of purest jet.
> I have a gentle cock . . .

I could not stifle my laughter. I hurriedly genuflected, left by a side door and stood outside composing myself until Sister Agnes joined me. I had heard her murmur that song many times in Latin during matins or vespers.

'Why did you show me that, mother?' I asked, wiping away my tears.

'To prove I am not Lady Prune Face's spy. Only you and Veronica know about that. Secondly,' the old nun tapped the side of her nose, 'we all know about you, Joanna of England, you can never keep a secret in a convent.' She grinned lopsidedly. 'Well, some secrets, but all the kingdom is talking about you and your lover. Do you really love him?' Sister Agnes prodded my belly. 'Do you want him deep inside you?' She lifted a hand, her first and second fingers intertwined. 'Do you want to be as one, like two flames which have come together?'

'You know I do, mother.'

'Then never give it up,' she said once again. 'Do not compromise. Do not negotiate. Accept no bribes, no lavish rewards. Don't end up like poor Agnes, sitting in a choir stall, staring up at long-gone dreams and clutching at shadows. We have one life, one love; they are linked. You can't have one without the other. Remember that, Joanna of England.' The old woman turned and proudly walked away.

How strange that I should receive such wise advice about love from an old nun! It comforted me. Why do lovers think that they love alone?

I left this letter and have now returned to it in the early hours of the morning. I woke to the blood pounding in my ears like the sea breaking on the shore. (Do you remember that day we took the castle children along the sea coast and watched the cogs and barges going down to the mouth of the Thames?) I couldn't sleep. Love burns in the mind; it is never faint, never cools, never dies. So why should my brain go quiet in its fleshy cell?

I rose and dressed and stared out through the shutters at my rose. I slipped sandals on my feet. The rain had fallen, gentle but persistent. In the cloisters puddles of water gazed up at me with cloudy eyes. I crossed the wet grass to my rose; my love for you went out like some lonely bird seeking its nest. I whispered to the rose how my eyes wanted to kiss your face. I think of you constantly. Love me with all you are, love me in all my being with all your being. Pray with me that, before I die, I discover the world behind your eyes. Never doubt me. Will I alter? Only when the sun dies. Will I falter? Not until eternity does. I need you as the earth needs rain and sunlight. My love for you will last till the earth cracks and the last nightingale chants its fleeting vespers for the final time.

I wish I could envelop your body like a vapour. I wake from wild dreams of you and my own dreadful nightmares. In one dream you were shrouded in the black wings of a huge bird; its head was shaped in the form of a falcon but its face was that of de Clare. Oh yes, he comes to me in the darkness of the night. De Clare, whose soul housed a thousand demons, with his dark looks and muttered curses, his elixirs, potions and Chamber of Shadows. I do not know which I resented the most, the de Clare who abused, beat and raped me or the dark-eyed, would-be sorcerer who searched for salvation. Perhaps in death he will find some peace from those phantasms which roused him soaked in sweat and screaming at ghosts I could never see. Only shortly before you were taken, when we became one, did I tell you the full truth behind my marriage. De Clare hid it so well, from you, his knights, even his would-be confessor Ricaud. My father never saw him as I did, the way he would suddenly stand up and talk to shadows, not only at night but even when the sun shone strong and full, at the entrance to a barn or a window overlooking the castle green. His red, gleaming hair would be soaked in sweat, his drinker's face florid and shimmering.

'See them!' he would yell at me. 'Do you see, Joanna, down there, grey shapes with blood-filled eyes and mouths!'

Sitting by that rain-dewed rose and thinking of you, the shadows lifted and the heat and warmth returned. I retired, peaceful, to my chamber and fell into a dreamless sleep.

When I wake in the morning I always try and forget my pain by thinking of the likes of Sister Agnes. I recall the words of the poetess Marie de France: 'Unrequited love is a body wound which has no outward sign.' I do not suffer alone, you do not suffer alone. I must take each day as it comes and lose myself in its routine duties.

Like you, I wonder how long this purgatory will last. Sometimes my panic is like a deadly contagion. In a sense my meeting with those royal archers offered a little hope. Father cannot keep this place ringed by so many armed men for ever and a day.

Three days ago the Lady Abbess sent a novice asking for my presence in her parlour. The Franciscan, Roger of Evesham was there, a man of authority, despite his brown robe, white girdle and sandalled feet. A strange priest, hair freshly cropped, sharp-featured. He was talking to the Lady Abbess in Norman French and caught my surprise when Lady Emma introduced me.

'We Franciscans,' he said, 'are no longer the poor men of Christ. We have among our brothers former soldiers, lawyers, clerks and merchants.' He took my hand and kissed it.

I noticed his right wrist was swathed in a clean white bandage.

'A burn,' he explained. 'I am not the best of cooks.'

He did not stand on idle ceremony. He studied me like a physician scrutinising the face of his patient and seemed to forget the Lady Emma; she coughed behind her hand to remind him of her presence. He turned to her and gave a slightly mocking bow.

'My lady, I do apologise. I would like to speak to the Lady Joanna alone.'

She was flustered. 'We have chambers. I . . . I . . . '

'No, no. God provides me with one. Let's walk in the garden, Lady Joanna.' He went to the door and put his hand on the latch.

'How long will you stay?' the Lady Abbess asked.

'How long is a piece of twine?' With that the friar opened the door and ushered me out.

I curbed my excitement; for the first time since my arrival here there was a shift in the balance. Father had intervened. The Franciscan Order, like their founder St Francis, refuses to pay even lip service to dignities and titles. The poor man of Assisi would have been proud of Brother Roger.

He grasped me by the elbow and steered me across the lawn to a stone seat. It was a cunning choice — no one could pretend they had something interesting to do nearby and eavesdrop.

'The Lady Abbess will be insulted,' I remarked.

'The Lady Abbess needs to be insulted,' Brother Roger retorted. 'Humility is an essential part of sanctity, and it is a virtue she sorely lacks.'

'Are you humble, Brother?'

'That is not for me to judge, Lady Joanna.'

'But you are my father's minion?'

'Like St Peter,' he quipped. 'I serve God and honour the King. The Franciscans are, how can I put it, well favoured by your father. Our house at Greyfriars near St Paul's provides both confessors and celebrants to the royal court.'

'And why are you here, Brother? To remind me of my duties to God and the King?'

A linnet in a tree across the lawn began to sing.

'We all must do what we have to do,' he said softly.

'Do you want to hear my confession, Brother?'

For the first time since I had met him he lost his poise. He sucked on his lower lip and shook his head. 'I have no power to do that, I am not the person . . . ' He edged closer, nursing his wounded wrist. 'I am going to ask you questions, my lady. If you do not wish to answer them, then you need not. If you believe I am impertinent then tell me so. I am here at your father's request but if you only wish to talk about that bird singing then that is what we shall discuss.'

I looked across at the bell tower of the church. I had vowed that I would tell our secret to no one. But if my father wanted to know the depth of my love for you then why should I refuse to talk to this friar? How could I sit silent like some sulky girl biting on her thumb?

'Will you report what I say to the King?'

Brother Roger nodded. 'Of course.'

'Why you, Brother? Why not some other friar?'

'You should ask your father that,' he said. 'But I tell you this, my lady, one day the full truth will be known.'

'What do you want to know, Brother? Has my father prepared a list of questions?'

'You are forthright,' he declared.

'Brother, when you are married to a man like de Clare, then fall in love with someone like Monthermer, you realise that being forthright, as you put it, is the only path open to you.' I could feel my temper rising. 'I felt as if I was being tossed from the frying pan into the fire. I married de Clare out of duty. Now, years on, I am being trotted out of the stable like a brood mare, for someone else to marry.'

'Is that how you feel, my lady?'

'No, Brother, that's the truth. I was a mere girl when I married de Clare. Imagine what it's like, Brother, to be a girl full of dreams? I thought marriage would be like heaven!'

I became so agitated, I got to my feet, wiping the sweat from my palms on my gown.

'Yes, I thought I was about to enter heaven only to discover I was imprisoned in the deepest chamber of hell!'

'So, you did not love de Clare?'

'You want the truth, Brother? Tell my father that I did not love de Clare. In fact I grew to hate him. I hated his smell, I hated his hair, I hated his hands. You are a priest who has taken a vow of chastity.' My voice hardened. 'Priests, in their ignorance, talk of holy marriage, of two bodies becoming one flesh. As Hell burns!' I swore. 'How can a man and a woman be one flesh when violence and torment stalk their union?'

'Did it start like that?'

'Of course not. De Clare was my father's premier general, keen-eyed and of noble appearance. But the veil does not make the nun. De Clare was two men: the noble earl and the bedroom tyrant. Can you imagine what it was like to be a girl romantic with milksop ideas and to live with a man who could only pierce you — that's how he described it — or beat you, or more usually both.'

'Yet you bore him three children.'

'And, God forgive me, Brother, but I shudder to recall their conception. It's not their fault, the little mites. As time passed, de Clare got worse, not better. I grew older, harder, like a soldier who has many times faced the battle line or a friar who has learned to endure kneeling for hours on the hard floor and eating nothing but plain bread and gruel. Eventually de Clare became impotent as his strange fancies took a stronger grip on his mind and soul. He built his Chamber of Shadows. He visited a local witch or wise woman. He became a prisoner of his past and my hatred turned to contempt. England's leading earl was nothing more than a wife-beater. No wonder his first wife begged Rome for an annulment!'

Brother Roger looked up at the sky.

'What are you looking for?' I taunted. 'Angels? Inspiration?'

'But you found a little peace?'

'Yes, in the shape of a long dagger. I told de Clare that if he touched me again, I would slice his throat while he was asleep and proclaim to the kingdom the reason I had done it. I discovered that de Clare had two fears: the past and the reckoning he would have to face on his death. He left me alone and I began to know some peace.'

'Did you blame your father for your marriage to such a man?'

'At first, yes, but de Clare was secretive. How could the King know? Oh, there were rumours . . . '

'You could have complained.'

'Could I, Brother?' I laughed. 'That's why you are here, isn't it? To remind me of my duty as a princess of England and daughter of the King. As de Clare's wife I wore that mask. But the older I grew, the greater I pitied him, and my husband began to hate me for it. The more distant and serene I became, the more intense his hatred grew.'

'Did you want him dead?'

I stared across at a wood pigeon which floated like a ghost down onto the lawn. This friar, I thought, is going to report back to the King. It was time my father knew the depths to which my marriage to de Clare had sunk.

'God forgive me, Brother,' I confessed, 'but, yes, I wanted him dead. Sometimes at night I would lie on my bed and pray that some arrow in a gloomy Welsh valley would take him in the throat or heart. A swift end to his agony, as well as to mine.'

'Then Ralph Monthermer arrived.'

'Yes, Brother, Ralph arrived. When I looked on his face, I realised how frozen my soul was and what it was like to enter the warmth.'

Brother Roger fidgeted with the knotted tassel of his girdle. 'Is that how you would describe it?' he asked. 'Coming out of the cold to a roaring fire? Is that really love? Or were you seeking rescue from your barren life and refuge from your husband?'

'Is that how you regard me, Brother, a thirsty woman ready to clutch at the first cup of water thrust into her hand? I tell you this, I had no time for the world of men. Oh, I had hot-eyed knights casting lecherous glances. Members of my husband's retinue paid gallant court, composed poems and begged to wear my colours in the lists. But in truth they were faceless, indeterminate shapes, hollow voices, empty glances. Ralph was different.'

'And one glance was enough?'

'Yes, Brother, one glance! Haven't you ever heard the saying, '*Ubi amor, ibi oculus* — where love is, there is the eye'? Or is it the other way round? I saw him and I loved him. You will say that I was hungry for love.'

'Well, weren't you?'

'If you travel on a long, cold journey and

you arrive at a tavern, you may embrace the warmth of the taproom fire all the more eagerly, but it is no less genuine for that. That was my feeling on first meeting Ralph. His face, his eyes, the way he smiled. I felt it in his first look and, God be my witness, he felt it in mine. I was coming home. I was at the door.'

Brother Roger looked up sharply. 'Why do you use the word home?'

'Because that is the way I felt, as if I had been travelling in a foreign land. He offered no false flattery or loud proclamations of devotion. He was not some court fop who came tripping into Tonbridge. In all things he was honourable. I welcomed him like a pious nun does the sacrament.'

'Some people would say such love was an illness.'

'Illness!' I laughed. 'Do I drip with sweat? Does palsy shake my limbs? Am I pale and withered like dry grass? I am not ill, Brother, and if Ralph were with me I would be complete. Every breath I breathe is a hint of him. My heart goes out to him like a bird flies towards its nest. He swept me back from the death-watch of life with love.' I could feel the blood beating within me. I just wished my father was there to hear my words for himself. 'I hated de Clare. I hated him for what he was and for what he had done but I did not fly to Ralph Monthermer like some moonstruck maid. I loved him!'

'You said you felt you were coming home,' Brother Roger repeated. 'Now, if you are coming home, you are returning to something. Have you ever loved anyone like you do Monthermer?'

I closed my eyes.

'Please answer,' the friar pressed. 'I wish to understand how you feel, my lady.'

'I love my father,' I said, 'and there is something of my father in Ralph, something of greatness, but it's more than that. I have never loved anyone like I love Ralph and I never will.'

Roger of Evesham sat chewing the corner of his lip, cradling his bandaged wrist. What had made me tell him how I felt? Would I have been as frank with the Lady Abbess had she shown the same interest? After all, this was the first time since the confrontation with my father in the chapel at Tonbridge that I had told another soul how I felt about you.

'You were married early, yes?'

I nodded.

Brother Roger got to his feet and smiled down at me. 'When I was in the Lady Abbess's chamber, she gave me a taste of wine.' He grinned. 'Claret any Franciscan would give his soul for. My lady, I will go and get a cup for you and me. In the meantime, please grant me one favour.'

'What favour?'

'Go back to the time when you were a child. Find for me your happiest, most peaceful memory.'

He did not wait for me to agree but walked across the lawn, humming softly beneath his breath. I was a little surprised because I recognised the tune, a madrigal rather than some pious hymn.

The sun had grown stronger. I turned to bask in its warmth. I was intrigued by the friar's request. Unlike you, I had a loving childhood; I and my siblings played like young puppies in the royal nursery. I recalled my father coming in and plucking me up.

'And how is my little squirrel?' he teased.

The image unlocked the door to the past. My father's shadow lies long across me; perhaps I expected Earl Gilbert to be like my father. After all, where do women gain their image of men? In my case not from little Edward my brother. No, it was always the Lion of England, Edward Plantagenet. But in my memories he was never alone. Behind him, beautiful, olive-skinned, with those dancing, slanted eyes, her golden hair falling down to her shoulders, was my mother. They were always together, constantly touching, smiling at each other. Tears of rage suddenly scalded my eyes. That is what I had expected from my marriage to de Clare!

'My lady?'

I opened my eyes. Brother Roger handed me a small silver-chased cup half-filled with wine. I blinked and sipped from it.

'When I was a little girl,' I began, 'my father always called me his squirrel. When I chewed food I'd push it into my cheeks. My hair wasn't so gold, rather reddish. I used to scurry about like a little animal. There was another reason. Have you ever watched a squirrel sit and stare? It is one of the few animals that seems intrigued by what goes on around it. I was fascinated by my parents. They were magnificent; the way they talked and laughed, their secret whispers, the way my father would murmur something into Eleanor's ear and this lovely blush appeared high on her cheeks before she lowered her head, as if shocked by his words. But her shoulders would be shaking with laughter. I used to love it when they came to see me.' I looked up and stared across the lawn.

'A priest once talked to me about angels and that is what I thought my parents were, great and gracious angels! One afternoon late in summer, we were staying in the royal palace at Winchester. My mother had her own private garden there, with trellised walks, flowered arbours, herb plots, a rose garden and a small fountain. Even the outside walls of the palace were decorated with climbing plants. Only my mother and my father were allowed in there. I used to watch them enter.' I sipped from the wine. 'One afternoon I stole in after them.'

'Like the little squirrel your father called you.'

'Yes. I took an apple to gnaw. I crept through the gate and hid beneath a great bush. I stayed there for an age, not moving, now and again taking a bite from the apple. So many years ago, yet I can taste that fruit now.'

'Why did you go there?'

'I wanted to see what my father and mother, these two golden angels, would do when they were alone. At last I heard them coming. My father's deep voice was singing a song, my mother was walking slightly ahead of him, holding the rose he had plucked for her. I have never seen anything as beautiful as that scene, my mother smiling over her shoulder and the great Edward of England softly teasing her. He tried to clutch her by the shoulder but she hurried on, laughing.'

I closed my eyes. I was no longer in the convent but in that garden staring bold-eyed and open-mouthed.

'My parents sat down among the flowers. I could see them clearly. Looking back, I realise they were playing a game. He was teasing her and she was acting coy. He moved closer and eventually they embraced. I had never seen my parents do that, kissing each other softly. My father lay down, put his head in my mother's lap and stared up at her and they talked, sometimes laughed. A few days later I was in my mother's chamber brushing her hair. I would do this sometimes. I would stand on a small footstool and she would watch me in the mirror.' I paused.

' 'What is it, squirrel?' my mother asked. 'Why do you stare at me so?'

'In my childish way I asked about her and father. She laughed and, turning on the chair, took me up and sat me in her lap.

' 'I love your father, he loves me, little squirrel.'

' 'And one day,' I asked, 'will someone love me like that. And will I love him?'

'My mother's face became sad. She reminded me of a picture of the Virgin after the crucified Christ has been laid in her arms. She pressed her cheek against my head.

' 'Pray,' she whispered. 'Pray, little one, that one day you will have the same love as I do.' '

Brother Roger put down his cup. 'And that's what you expected from your marriage to de Clare?'

'I hoped for it, certainly. And when I met Ralph, as I have said, it was like coming home.'

'Your husband must have been aware of this.'

'De Clare had a sick soul. There's a Spanish proverb, Brother: 'Revenge is a dish best served cold.' Ralph Monthermer was his revenge. I could see it in his mocking eyes, challenging me to sin, enjoying my torment when I resisted.'

'Did you resist, my lady?'

'Before de Clare's death, I committed no sin, though God knows the temptation was strong.'

Brother Roger drained his cup and put it down between his feet. 'Will you swear to that, my lady?'

'I will.'

'You were a married woman. De Clare was an obstacle. It would be only human for you and Sir Ralph to plot against him.'

'Plot what, Brother?'

He raised his eyebrows. 'There are rumours,

allegations even, that Sir Ralph had a hand in Earl Gilbert's death.'

Oh, my golden hawk, my heart went cold. You had warned me of the whispers but rumours are common enough when any person dies in mysterious or violent circumstances. What was this friar saying? That malicious chatter had some standing in law?

'My lady, you have paled.'

'Sir Ralph is as innocent as I am of Earl Gilbert's death!'

'Do you know what happened in the Chamber of Shadows that night?'

'No, I do not.'

'Did you know the woman Malherbes?'

'Yes, Brother, I did. I visited her on a number of occasions. In the time before I met Sir Ralph I needed strong potions to help me sleep, to soothe the humours.'

'Were you glad when Earl Gilbert died?'

'I am happy for no man's death. But I am no hypocrite. I could not grieve or weep.'

'Even though your children had lost their father?'

'He despised them as much as he despised me. Earl Gilbert had time for no one but himself.'

Brother Roger leaned forward, elbows on his knees, hands clasped together as if in prayer. I wondered how busy he had been on this matter.

'I think you know more than you pretend, Brother,' I said.

He repressed a smile. 'I know nothing except what a clerk of the Royal Chapel, a Master Henry Trokelowe, has told me.'

'Oh yes, I know of him. He is one of my father's limners, a greyhound sent out to bring the quarry down.'

Brother Roger coloured slightly and refused to meet my eye.

'What is being hunted?' he asked.

'Why, Brother, that is obvious enough. Sir Ralph and I are the buck and the doe cut out from the herd.'

'I don't think so,' he replied so fiercely he startled me.

'Why, what do you hunt then?'

'The truth.'

'I have told you the truth. God forgive me, I love Sir Ralph. I wish to be with him. I will not marry anyone else. I am prepared to give up Gloucester and England. I would walk to the nearest port in my shift, as long as Sir Ralph was beside me.'

'But what about your children?'

'My children, eventually, will understand and love me for what I am, not what Earl Gilbert and my father forced me to become.'

'So you did not lie with Sir Ralph before your husband's death?'

'I have already said so.'

'And although you wished Earl Gilbert's death, you did not plot it?'

'No.'

'And you believe Sir Ralph to be innocent of it?'

'I would swear to it.'

'He is a penniless Welsh Knight,' said Brother Roger, suddenly changing tack, as if he hoped to unsettle me, like a lawyer would an unreliable witness. 'How do you know that he loves you, that he was not simply seeking his fortune through you?'

I grasped the friar's left wrist and dug my nails into his skin until he winced. 'Have you ever loved, Brother?'

'I love Christ.'

'What do you mean by that?' I asked, remembering my conversation with the Lady Abbess. 'How can you love what you cannot see? Do you wish to embrace Christ and kiss him on the lips?'

He did not look shocked.

'Some people might say that was blasphemy,' he murmured.

'But men did,' I answered. 'Judas put his arms round him and kissed him in Gethsemane.'

'Aye, but he was betraying him.'

'And Jesus knew that,' I declared. 'That's the thing about love, Brother, it cannot lie. You say you love Christ whom you cannot see. I am sure that you will take an oath that you do not lie.' I released my grip. 'I love Sir Ralph whom I can see. I know by his eyes, by his mouth, in my innermost being, that Ralph loves me as much as I do him.'

'What would have happened if de Clare had not fallen down those steps?'

'Then as God is my witness I would not have continued to live as his wife. Earl Gilbert de Clare's first marriage had been annulled by Rome, why not his second?'

'You would have done that? Because of Monthermer?'

'No, Brother, because of me.'

'On what grounds?'

'The Church teaches that a marriage must be entered into freely and with full knowledge. I would have sworn an oath that had I known what de Clare was really like, I would rather have taken vows as a nun and buried myself in the loneliest convent than share his bed.'

'And who advised you on this, my lady? Some priest, some lawyer?'

'The parish priest of the Church of St John, a good, kindly man. He was my confessor. He knew my pain. He would have helped me.'

'You confided in Father Benedict?'

'He was my confessor.' I looked at the sky. The day was changing, dark clouds were approaching from the coast. 'I have answered your questions, Brother Roger. Now you can answer mine. What is my father's mind in this?'

'I do not know.'

Again I caught the friar by the wrist. 'Tell my father I will not marry the man of his choice, Amadeus of Savoy, or anyone else. Tell him that if he forces me to stay here, I will try to escape, and if I succeed I will proclaim to the world what de Clare was. I will appeal to Holy Mother Church for protection. I will fight for myself, for Sir Ralph Monthermer and for my children. The king is my father but my life and my will are God-given. I will not be forced to do what, in conscience, I cannot do.'

The friar shifted uneasily as if taken aback by the force of my words. I was pleased. I wanted this messenger to understand and convey to my father the strength of my convictions.

'And if the King released you?' Brother Roger asked.

'I would travel immediately to Ralph.'

'And what would you feel?'

'I would be at one with him, Brother. I would have harmony. I would know peace and I would know love. I would get down on my knees and thank God, as my mother told me to. Tell my father that.'

Brother Roger examined the bandage round his wrist. 'Such passion,' he murmured. 'You need not answer this, my lady, but if you committed no sin before Earl Gilbert's death, what about afterwards? Did you lie with Sir Ralph?'

I felt myself colour; my stomach twisted, my heart lurched.

'You need not answer, my lady.'

'I need not and I shall not. If my father wishes to know that then let him travel here and ask me himself, face to face. Let him stand before me, not as King of England, but as my father and hear what I have to say.'

'My lady, he will not do that.'

I felt the cool breeze on my face and realised how hot and flushed the wine had made me. I was glad I had spoken as I had. This subtle friar would collect my words like pieces of bread in a basket and take them to my father, and he would know the truth. He would have known before now but for his fiery outburst at Tonbridge.

Brother Roger got to his feet and stared down at me. 'My lady.' He took my hand

and kissed it. 'I must leave now. Do you have any message for the King?'

'Yes, say that I love him. Aye, and tell him I envy him for what he had.' I kept my voice steady. 'I do not hate him because he deprives me of what he had with my mother. You will say that, Brother?'

The friar nodded and smiled. 'And your love for Sir Ralph will not change as long as the earth stays green.'

'Yes, tell my father that.'

Brother Roger felt inside his habit and handed me a parchment. My heart skipped. I flushed with pleasure as I recognised your sweet hand and the seal attached to it.

'Have you met Ralph?'

But Brother Roger was already walking away. I did not really care. It would not have mattered if St Michael and all his angels had left heaven to visit me. I broke the seal. The parchment was long, your handwriting small, the ink uneven, indicating where you had stopped and started.

I read the middle first, then the end and went back to the beginning. I am not too sure how long I sat there. The two old ones, Sister Agnes and Sister Veronica, came across but I was hardly aware of them. You were mine and I was yours. That piece of parchment contained my life, it was the centre of my existence. My pleasure at reading it was like the calm surface of a lake, beneath which my soul grew cold at the tricks played upon you by the lawyer Cordell and the allegations levelled against you. The arrival of Trokelowe clearly heralds a different approach, but I cannot discern from his questions what my father intends.

Eventually I joined the sisters in the refectory but I sat like a ghost looking at my food. Early this evening, I returned to my chamber to continue this letter. Outside in the cloister garth a bird sang. I stared down at our rose but now it, too, is beginning to fade as if in sympathy with the day. The shadows grow longer, I feel so cold without you. I do not know how long I can tolerate this imprisonment.

I returned to your letter and, once again, my mood changed. We have kept our secret but I think Trokelowe and Brother Roger play a sly game. We must be careful of what we write. I re-examined the seal at both ends of your letter. Had it been broken before? Has the cipher been translated? Why did Brother Roger talk about my love lasting as long as the earth is green? Did I not say something like that in my first letter to you? And how did he know about Father Benedict being parish priest of St John's?

There is also a curious similarity between the questions Trokelowe asked you and those Brother Roger asked me. Yet, in truth, I do not care. Let the world go hang and let my father know that my every breath is for you, every beat of my heart sings your name. If I cannot live with you then I shall not live without you.

I cannot write any more. I cannot tell you how close my heart is to breaking.

Written at Malmesbury, the feast of St Columba, June 1297.

Letter 8

Henry Trokelowe, former clerk of the Royal Chapel, to Edward the King, health and greetings.

I have, as Your Grace knows, refused your summons to present myself at Westminster. Instead, I have taken sanctuary in Christchurch Priory, Canterbury. Past its main gates winds the white chalky road down to the port of Dover.

When I entered your service, I took a solemn oath before Christ and his saints, my hand resting on a Book of the Gospels, to give you good counsel. I am also, as Your Grace knows, skilled in the law. I know that behind the will of a prince lies the rigour of the law and that the anger of a prince can mean death. I am not a coward but neither am I a brave man. I am certainly not foolish. You asked me to investigate the matter concerning your daughter and I have done so. I can do no more than tell the truth and in all conscience I believe your daughter deserves the same and I attach a copy of the letter I have despatched to her.

Now, what is the truth? Let us take Gilbert

de Clare, Earl of Gloucester. Oh, Your Grace, he was well named the Red Earl. A leading nobleman, your premier general, de Clare may have had many virtues though none that I can see. He had the morals of an alley bully. He was a murderer at heart and loved no one but himself. Many years ago he massacred a group of Jews — men, women and children — and this heinous sin came back to haunt him. It soured an already sour life. He was married once and that marriage was annulled. For reasons of state, and the security of your realm, his second bride was your daughter, the Lady Joanna. In truth, and I will speak *ex corde*, from the heart, I would not have married him to my dog let alone my daughter. De Clare was mean-spirited and narrow-minded. His idea of love was power, ambition and conquest.

You have seen copies of the letters that passed between Sir Ralph and the Lady Joanna. My scribe Wimborne can unlock any cipher and was able to read the letters with the greatest of ease. He broke the cipher and transcribed them, then replicated the seal. All it took was a matter of a few hours before the original was despatched on its way. Wimborne is not to be blamed for my present decision, Your Grace knows him well. The poor scribe wiped that ever-dripping nose of his and made his confession. He told me, 'Where you go, Master Trokelowe, I follow. If you fear the King's wrath, then so do I.'

Wimborne is with me at Christchurch. He, too, intends to seek sanctuary abroad. However, I digress: the Earl of Gloucester. Marriages may be made in heaven but some are planned in hell. The one between Lady Joanna and Earl Gilbert was, for your daughter, a living nightmare. Let her words speak for themselves. I believe she tells the truth; I have found no evidence to the contrary. The Lady Joanna is to be praised for her honesty and lack of guile.

As for the Earl's death, I can lay no blame with either Sir Ralph or the Lady Joanna. Earl Gilbert ignored the teaching of Holy Mother Church and dabbled in rites no sane man would ever consider. He believed he could use the black arts to exorcise his own demons; in doing so he brought about his own death. On the night he died, Earl Gilbert had ordered the woman Malherbes to summon a demon. Remember her words, that those who venture too close to the darkness on the edge of life imperil their souls. That night Earl Gilbert stepped too close, and something from the darkness made its presence felt. Earl Gilbert, dishevelled, probably in his cups, could not cope with it. He fled in panic from his chamber. He reached the top of the steps and, in his drunken fear, simply slipped and fell to his death.

We have the evidence of witnesses that Earl Gilbert would allow no one inside that chamber, except Malherbes who on the night in question fled from that unearthly place. Lady Joanna was in her own chamber with her maid Alicia. As for Sir Ralph, Malherbes stated quite clearly that, as she left the castle, she passed Sir Ralph on his way to the Chamber of Shadows. As far as I can determine, Earl Gilbert died very shortly after her rapid departure. I believe he went to follow but fell to his death. Sir Ralph found his corpse and raised the alarm. I am sure that if Sir Ralph had climbed those steps to confront Earl Gilbert and provoke a quarrel over the Lady Joanna, de Clare would have drawn his dagger. There would have been a struggle and the alarm would have been raised. Your Grace, I swear, there is not a shred of evidence that this occurred.

Now, as for the Earl Gilbert's marriage to your daughter, it was a sham and a mockery. The Lady Joanna entered it full of hope but this soon turned to hate. She eventually refused to share her bed with the Earl and threatened the direst consequences, including public shame and humiliation if he offered further abuse. Earl Gilbert, a man full of arrogance, had no choice but to accept. And why not? The fears which possessed him grew by the day and made him as impotent as any gelding. Instead he cast about and time provided him with the means for revenge. He led your armies in Wales and was taken by the young squire Monthermer who returned with him to Tonbridge. I believe the Lady Joanna truly had had enough of the world of men, be it de Clare or, indeed, any man on the face of God's earth except for one: Ralph Monthermer. By God's good grace or by the sheerest luck, Lady Joanna met the love of her life. In one glance, in one meeting, she recognised that. And why is this so? True, I have studied the writings of Constantine the African on lovesickness as well as the treatises of other different scholars. I now realise that their principal error is their theory of the sameness of love, like some contagion which can spread from one man to another. Love is not like that. In every relationship it is unique. It sparks its own fire and burns differently in one than it does in the other.

Let us take the Lady Joanna. She is your daughter and that of Eleanor of Castile. She is beautiful, comely in face and body.

She shares your virtues and vices. She is hot-headed, impetuous, strong-willed and, once her mind is fixed, ruthless in any decision she makes. De Clare experienced that ruthlessness and avoided her. The Lady Joanna is formidable, be it in hate or love. She is intelligent and reflective. She was raised in a family where she witnessed love at its most intense, between yourself and the late Queen Eleanor. Lady Joanna experienced love as a child in all its allure and, as a young woman, looked for it herself. De Clare could never, even if he'd lived till the world had cracked, have offered even the slightest shred of this. Perhaps the Lady Joanna would have met some other? Instead she met a fellow soul. Someone who responded to her own idea of love. Is it so strange that her love for Monthermer knows no bounds? Like a dam brimming with water and Monthermer was the man to break it. So the Lady Joanna will not change, she will never give him up. Despite all my learning, I recognised Lady Joanna's love for Monthermer is simple and pure in its intensity, all powerful in its effect.

And Monthermer? In Mathematics they say like responds to like. To all intents and purposes Monthermer is a Welsh squire, a man raised and trained in a house of war.

But he, too, shared the same flame as the Lady Joanna. He had not experienced love but he had an idea, like a reflection in a dull mirror, of what it should be. Lady Joanna made this clear to him. Like answered like. Both flames fed on each other. I doubt even death itself can dampen the raging fire which has ensued.

And how did they act? Lady Joanna and Sir Ralph no doubt loved each other in thought and word but, before de Clare's death, never in deed. The Lady Joanna knew Earl Gilbert's soul. She would refuse to be trapped, to have her love for Monthermer, and his for her, be turned like a sword against both of them. In this they were truly innocent. Instead, Lady Joanna, with her sharp wit and iron will, decided to play the game back. She would not be depicted as an adulteress. She would not allow Monthermer to be disgraced as a knight. She would do that which was honest and open. She sought the advice of her confessor Father Benedict and, if de Clare had lived, would undoubtedly have approached you to seek an annulment from Rome. In her eyes, de Clare's death must have appeared as an act of God. I doubt if the Lady Joanna could truly believe that the Earl Gilbert was dead. Did she fear his ghost? Is that why she protected her room? She kept her dagger beneath her pillow, as if she really believed that, one night, Earl Gilbert would come tapping on her door again.

Lady Joanna donned widow's weeds. She was not loud in her grief, refusing to act the hypocrite. The life of the castle continued. She and Sir Ralph became closer, often journeying down to see their confessor and adviser Father Benedict in the Church of St John. This only added to the jealousy and spite of Ricaud the priest and Tibault the seneschal. These two limbs of Satan were the cause and origin of the scurrilous gossip and malicious chatter which would eventually tarnish the reputation of both your daughter and Sir Ralph.

Their correspondence refers, time and again, to their great secret. At first, God forgive me, I believed this was a reference to Earl Gilbert's death. However, when I was satisfied this could not be so, I recalled the love poetry, the hair fillet a widow should never wear, the ring and, above all, that painting in St John's Church at Tonbridge. I journeyed back down to Tonbridge and surprised the venerable priest, Father Benedict, in his little house behind the church.

'Master Henry!' he exclaimed, his eyes

guarded. 'What brings you back to this place?'

'Why, Father, your church.'

The smile of welcome faded. 'The tomb of Earl Gilbert?'

'Father, I am no more interested in Lord Gilbert's tomb than you are. No, it is the painting in the Lady Chapel that draws me back.'

He sighed and sat down on a stool in his small stone-paved kitchen. 'I cannot tell you,' he whispered.

'I am not asking you to, Father. I simply wish to see it again.'

He took the ring of keys from a hook near the small dole cupboard in the wall and led me into the church through the coffin door. It was late afternoon. I thrust a silver piece into his hand and lit every candle in the Lady Chapel, pushing the iron stand closer so I could see the painting in every detail.

'What fascinates me about this, Father, is that here are a man and woman in what is supposed to be a bedchamber. Their faces could be anybody's but I suspect the lady represents Joanna and the man Sir Ralph. It is some time since I saw it last, but over the last few days I have given it careful thought. Why are their slippers and boots not on their feet but pushed aside?'

'Because it's a bedchamber,' the priest replied.

'No. I think it's a holy place,' I told him. 'It is written in the Book of Exodus that when God spoke to Moses, he said, 'Put off the shoes on your feet, for the place where you stand is holy ground.' ' I pointed to the roundels of the passion, the prayer beads, the statue of St Margaret.

'Decorations,' said Father Benedict defensively.

'And why is one candle lit, even though it is midday in the scene? Does not the single candle signify the presence of Christ?'

Father Benedict now looked very uncomfortable.

'And there are other symbols and clues,' I continued. 'The lady stands close to the bed. St Margaret is one of the patronesses of a happy marriage.' I pointed to the crouching dog. 'Is that not a symbol of fidelity? The fruit is a symbol of paradise, of Eden, where Adam and Eve exchanged their first vows. And these two figures in the mirror. They are not a reflection of the man and woman. I suggest they are the vague shapes of two witnesses: yourself and Lady Joanna's maid Alicia.'

I turned to look at Father Benedict.

'According to canon law, Father, when a

man and woman are married, the marriage certificate, or charter, must be signed by the parish priest. I believe this painting is the marriage certificate of the Lady Joanna and Sir Ralph. This is their great secret, is it not?'

The priest shifted and looked at the painting.

'Father, I know church law,' I persisted. 'For a man and woman to be married, there must be at least two witnesses, one of whom can be the priest. A document must be sworn, signed and sealed in the sanctuary of the church where they are married, officially declaring that they are now husband and wife. Lady Joanna had her mind set on this, didn't she? After all, she was free to marry and so was Sir Ralph.'

The priest bowed his head and stared down at the floor.

'It wasn't only the painting, Father.' I continued kindly. 'I discovered love poetry, a ring and conflicting testimony.'

'What do you mean?'

'Well, the maid Alicia was prepared to take an oath that, after Earl Gilbert's death, Lady Joanna and Sir Ralph committed no sin. Yet the woman Malherbes saw them lie as man and wife, deep in the woods between here and the castle. Lady Joanna and Sir Ralph were willing to talk of their feelings for each other before the Earl's death, but they refused to discuss their relationship after his death, except to say they committed no sin. And you, Father, were just as reticent on the matter.'

I stared at the painting again.

'What does it mean? I wondered. Alicia is not lying, Lady Joanna is not lying. The same goes for Sir Ralph and Father Benedict. But what about the testimony of Malherbes and the great secret Lady Joanna and Sir Ralph refer to in their correspondence?'

'You intercepted their letters?' Father Benedict interrupted tersely.

'I had no choice, Father. Anyway, I reached the conclusion that the only solution to all these riddles was that the Lady Joanna and Sir Ralph were already husband and wife. Earl Gilbert died in December, didn't he? Lady Joanna and Sir Ralph had no doubts about their love for each other. They came here and talked to you. You agreed to the marriage but advised them to exercise great prudence. In the castle Lady Joanna had to act the widowed Countess of Gloucester, Sir Ralph her squire. But here in this church they became one in holy matrimony and their wedding chamber was in Tonbridge woods.'

Father Benedict got to his feet and started blowing out the candles.

'You are a clever man, Trokelowe. When you first came here I looked into your sharp eyes and thought here is a man who will ferret out the truth.' He turned to face me squarely. 'I might as well tell you as be taken to London to tell the King. Lady Joanna and Sir Ralph did come to me. They had committed no sin. They were deeply in love and free to marry, so what could I do? Alicia was also party to their secret and took a most solemn oath on the matter. I married them here one morning before dawn and shared the wedding cup with them. They are husband and wife, Master Trokelowe, one flesh, and what God has joined together, let no man put asunder.' He gestured at the painting and smiled. 'Lady Joanna insisted on this. 'I want some sign, I want some symbol,' she declared. 'A discreet record of what has happened.' She sent for the wandering painter. I suspect he knew what he was doing; he worked as long as light lasted, was well paid, then went on his way.'

I recalled the love poem I had found written in a different hand in Monthermer's chamber and told the priest about it.

'I wrote that out for him,' said Father

Benedict. 'It was Sir Ralph's poem which he wished to recite on their wedding morning.' He straightened his shoulders. 'What will happen now? Will the King use his power and have the Archbishop of Canterbury send envoys to Rome?'

'I don't know, Father.'

'Will you tell the King?'

'I must,' I replied, 'but it's the truth that I seek, not injury to Lady Joanna or to Sir Ralph.'

So there, Your Grace, you have it. Your daughter and Monthermer are joined in a valid sacrament of marriage. Father Benedict is correct, you may appeal to Rome, but will His Holiness unlock a bond formed in heaven and blessed by God? And why should you do this? In God's name, why deny your daughter the happiness that you had in such measure during your marriage to the Lady Eleanor? What is wrong with her love? What objection to Monthermer? That he is base-born? He possesses more honour and ability in his little finger than Earl Gilbert had in his entire body.

I beg you, do not visit your wrath upon Sir Ralph or Lady Joanna but upon me for my bluntness and forthright speech. I fear your wrath, hence my stay in sanctuary. If you so wish, I will travel abroad and you will be done with me. I ask only for a Chancery writ of safe conduct to the port of Dover for both myself and Winborne who insists that where I go, he will follow. In the end, however, all I have done is what a good servant should have done. I have made diligent search. I have sifted fact from rumour. I have discovered the truth, not only for Your Grace but for myself. I have honoured my oath to you: I have kept faith.

Written at Christchurch, Canterbury, the feast of St Ethelreda, June 1297.

Letter 9

From Henry Trokelowe to Lady Joanna, Princess of England, Countess of Gloucester, health and greetings.

I write to confess and seek your absolution because your pardon is more important to me than that of your father.

First, it was my idea to allow you and Sir Ralph to correspond. I did it because I wished to discover the truth. Your letters were intercepted, your cipher translated and the letters re-sealed in a matter of hours. I have intruded and for that I beg your pardon.

Your letters demonstrate the great love between yourself and Sir Ralph. Such a love should not be hidden away. You have borne injury and great insult in the name of duty and for the sake of your father. You should not have to do it again. If I can be of service to you as a witness to that nightmare of a marriage to Earl Gilbert or as a champion of the love between yourself and Sir Ralph, it would gladden my heart.

You are a woman of sharp wit. It was only a matter of time before you realised that Roger of Evesham and Henry Trokelowe were one and the same person. I had my hair shorn, a white bandage put round my wrist and wore a Franciscan robe and girdle. Your assessment of me in your letter to Sir Ralph suggested you would not speak to one such as Henry Trokelowe, and who can blame you? Brother Roger of Evesham, perhaps, was a more sympathetic figure. Please think of it as a piece of mummery and accept my word that it did your cause only good, since I was pursuing the truth, nothing else. You and Sir Ralph are deeply in love. You are totally innocent of any involvement in Earl Gilbert's death. You did not seek or take his life. May God have mercy on his tortured soul.

I have also visited Father Benedict and studied your painting. I know that you and Sir Ralph are joined in holy matrimony, which not even your father can break. I am now in sanctuary, in fear of your father's wrath because I have told him that in my opinion you and Sir Ralph should be allowed to live your lives free and untrammelled. Moreover, I have taken him to task for denying to you what he so enjoyed with your late lamented mother Eleanor of Castile. God knows what the King will make of it.

Finally, I am writing because I wish to thank you for completing my education. I am skilled in treatises, I have studied all the theories on love and the sickness it purportedly causes. They are nothing but dust in the wind. I once loved a man, as a brother. He fell in love and lost not only the love of his life but life itself. Now I know that love is unique, a special flame which burns in each of us. Sometimes, if we are lucky, that flame flares up to meet its match, and two souls, two hearts, two minds, two bodies become one. Love does not see defects only virtues. It has no limits but stretches into eternity. It accepts all and forgives all. It is not a sickness but a God-given gift. It is when we love that we become fully human and, being fully human, become divine.

So, Joanna of England, may your love for Sir Ralph touch the King's soul as it has mine, and bring you the fulfilment you deserve.

Written at Christchurch, Canterbury, the feast of St Ethelreda, June 1297.

Letter 10

From Edward, King of England, to Hugh Bigod, Earl of Norfolk and Marshal of England, health and greetings.

It is our clear wish that, on receipt of this letter, you immediately take a force of knight bannerets and proceed urgently to our castle at Bristol. Using our authority, you are to arrange the immediate release of Sir Ralph Monthermer imprisoned there. He is a free man on whom the law has no demands. He is to be treated as our son-in-law and provided with fitting apparel, weapons and horses.

While in Bristol, you are to thank Sir Miles Sempringham for his care of Monthermer and inform the city council that the notary, Master Cordell, is no longer retained by the Crown. You are then to proceed immediately, with Monthermer, to the Convent of St Mary at Malmesbury.

You will seek an urgent audience with Lady Emma the Abbess and order her to release into your hands our well-beloved daughter, Joanna, Princess of England and Countess of Gloucester. Our daughter Joanna is to be informed that she, too, is free of any demands under the law. She is to be shown every courtesy and allowed to travel in your retinue with her husband Sir Ralph. They are to be given every respect and honour and brought to meet us at our palace at Eltham.

Before leaving the convent, you are to carry out the following tasks. You are to order the Lady Abbess to give honourable burial to any remains of the woman Philippa atte Churche who allegedly committed suicide there during our good father's reign. You are to instruct the Lady Abbess to be more fair in her discipline and to provide reading which will humour, as well as educate, the good sisters in her care. You are to thank Lady Emma for her care of our well-beloved daughter then seek out two venerable sisters, known by their convent names, Veronica and Agnes. You are to provide each of them with a purse of one hundred pounds sterling. You shall instruct the Lady Abbess that each of these good sisters be allowed to order a stained-glass window of their choice opposite their stalls in the convent church. The cost of glaziers and painters is, of course, to be forwarded to our exchequer in London.

Once you have delivered our well-beloved daughter and son-in-law to our palace of

Eltham, you are to proceed to Christchurch Priory on the outskirts of Canterbury. You shall seek Father Prior's permission to approach our well-beloved clerk of the Royal Chapel, Henry Trokelowe, who, in the mistaken belief that he has incurred our wrath, is sheltering in sanctuary. You shall deliver the following message:

'Edward of England to his well-beloved clerk of the Royal Chapel, Henry Trokelowe, now residing in Christchurch Priory, Canterbury, health and greetings.

'Upon my solemn oath, and I shall never repent of it, your presence at our chambers at Westminster is sorely missed. We urgently seek your good advice and counsel on a number of outstanding matters. You are mistaken in thinking that you have incurred our wrath. I set you to discover the truth and, like a good and loyal servant, you have done so. You have offered me good counsel and advice which the Earl Marshal of England will swear, on holy relics, I have accepted. You are to return immediately to Westminster and fresh duties in the Royal Chapel. In the meantime I have ordered the refurbishment of your boat at King's Steps, Westminster and issued a writ, under the Great Seal, granting Henry Trokelowe,

Clerk, the manor of Bisham in Oxford and all fishing rights thereto.'

Given at Westminster and despatched under the Secret Seal on the feast of St Thomas, July 1297.

Postscript

This is a love story from history. Edward I was passionately in love with his first wife Eleanor of Castile and was distraught when she died. The chroniclers of the day remark that Edward was never the same after Eleanor's death; even today, at Charing Cross, there is a monument to Edward's great love for 'his lady of Castile'.

Medieval philosophers were fascinated by what they termed lovesickness and Henry Trokelowe's studies reflect the thinking of the time.

Edward I's rage against his daughter is well documented. Both she and Sir Ralph had to face temporary disgrace and confinement in the spring and summer of 1297. Edward abruptly relented. Joanna's marriage to Sir Ralph, who was later created Earl of Gloucester, was accepted by King and Church. It was a love affair which lasted for the rest of their lives. Joanna died on 23 April 1307 and Ralph in 1326. She and Sir Ralph had two sons and a daughter.

Henry Trokelowe died as he had lived, a bachelor.

VANESSA ALEXANDER

We do hope that you have enjoyed reading this large print book.

Did you know that all of our titles are available for purchase?

We publish a wide range of high quality large print books including:
Romances, Mysteries, Classics
General Fiction
Non Fiction and Westerns

Special interest titles available in large print are:
The Little Oxford Dictionary
Music Book
Song Book
Hymn Book
Service Book

Also available from us courtesy of Oxford University Press:
Young Readers' Dictionary
(large print edition)
Young Readers' Thesaurus
(large print edition)

For further information or a free brochure, please contact us at:
Ulverscroft Large Print Books Ltd.,
The Green, Bradgate Road, Anstey,
Leicester, LE7 7FU, England.
Tel: (00 44) 0116 236 4325
Fax: (00 44) 0116 234 0205

THE VILLA VIOLETTA

June Barraclough

In the 1950s, Xavier Leopardi returned to Italy to reclaim his dead grandfather's beautiful villa on Lake Como. Xavier's English girlfriend, Flora, goes to stay there with him and his family, but finds the atmosphere oppressive. Xavier is obsessed with the memory of his childhood, which he associates with the scent of violets. There is a mystery concerning his parents and Flora is determined to solve it, in her bid to 'save' Xavier from himself. Only after much sorrow will Edwige, the old housekeeper, finally reveal what happened there.

THE WORLD AT NIGHT

Alan Furst

Jean Casson, a well-dressed, well-bred Parisian film producer, spends his days in the finest cafes and bistros, his evenings at elegant dinner parties and nights in the apartments of numerous women friends — until his agreeable lifestyle is changed for ever by the German invasion. As he struggles to put his world back together and to come to terms with the uncomfortable realities of life under German occupation, he becomes caught up — reluctantly — in the early activities of what was to become the French Resistance, and is faced with the first of many impossible choices.

ISLAND OF FLOWERS

Jean M. Long

'Swallowfield' had belonged to Bethany Tyler's family for generations, but now Aunt Sophie, who lived on Jersey, was claiming her share of the property. It seemed that the only way of raising the capital was to sell the house, but then, unexpectedly, Justin Rochel arrived in Sussex and things took on a new dimension. Bethany accompanied her father and sister to Jersey, where there were shocks in store for her. She was attracted to Justin, but could she trust him?

LAND OF MY DREAMS

Kate North

Maisie, an elderly lady, has lived in the shadow of her domineering and reclusive mother. Now her mother is dead and Maisie finally has a chance at life — one she comes to see and to experience through her new neighbours, the recently bereaved Clare and her teenage son, Joe. The unlikeliest of friendships begins as Joe, acting almost instinctively, draws Maisie out of her shell. Gradually, the secret that kept Maisie and her mother on the move and away from society is revealed, and Maisie finds the strength to make one last bid for happiness.